KHERIS BURNING

THIEVES' GUILD ORIGINS
LC BOOK ONE

The Thieves' Guild Books
by C.G. Hatton

Residual Belligerence #1
Blatant Disregard #2
Harsh Realities #3
Wilful Defiance #4
Darkest Fears #5
Arunday's Convergence #6

Kheris Burning LC#1
Beyond Redemption LC#2
Defying Winter LC#3

www.cghatton.com

KHERIS BURNING

THIEVES' GUILD ORIGINS
LC BOOK ONE

C.G. HATTON

First published in paperback in 2016
by Sixth Element Publishing
Arthur Robinson House
13-14 The Green
Billingham TS23 1EU
www.6epublishing.net

© C.G. Hatton 2016

ISBN 9798414858645

C.G. Hatton asserts the moral right to be identified as the author of this work.

British Library Cataloguing in Publication Data. A catalogue record for this book is available from the British Library.

All rights reserved. No part of this publication may be reproduced, stored in a retrieval system or transmitted, in any form or by any means, electronic, mechanical, photocopying, recording and/or otherwise without the prior written permission of the publishers. This book may not be lent, resold, hired out or disposed of by way of trade in any form, binding or cover other than that in which it is published without the prior written consent of the publishers.

For Hatt

With special thanks to...
Lynn Jackson, Clare Kent, Andrew and Eli Williams, Ste Baker, Jonathan and Aaron Fletcher, John Holmes-Carrington, Nathan Reynolds, Andy Harness and Steve Dickinson at Sci-Fi Scarborough, Gary Erskine, Bruce Connelly in New York and, as always, Graeme at 6E, Jan, Dave and my mum, and very special thanks to Hatt and the munchkins.

1

"You want to know what it takes to get to the top of the most secretive guild in the galaxy? Luck. That's it. Train and sweat and study all you want but in the end it pretty much comes down to luck. But you know the funny thing about luck? You have to make it. I learned that the hard way. When I was a kid on the streets of Kheris."

I can't help but stare at him. He hasn't changed, not really. His voice is quiet but everyone is listening. It's as if nothing else is happening. I sit on the stairs and hug my knees, watching as he tells his story, our story.

"We didn't know what they were all fighting over on our hellhole of a mining colony on the edge of the Between," he says, looking up to catch my eye, *"why the roads were blocked by tanks, why there was never any food in the shops, why they dropped bombs on us every night. We didn't know and we didn't care. But I do know one thing... everything changed the night something huge fell out of jump too close to the planet and crashed in our desert."*

He looks around at them all. *"But that wasn't the only thing that happened in those few weeks just before my fourteenth birthday. What happened first, and what saved my life in the end, was that Charlie came back..."*

A rocket screamed overhead. I didn't stop, reckoned I could make it and ran. The massive bulk of the remote weapons installation swung round with no warning.

I was too close to the edge. I think I stopped breathing. It felt like the world slipped into slow motion. The huge mass of the weapon's main housing punched down as it pounded one of its massive bolts out into the sky to intercept the rocket. I couldn't move fast enough, trying to shift my ass out of the way and not lose my balance, flinching from the heat, the noise. I was too close. The exhaust port scraped past me. Pain flared in my arm. I was knocked sideways and I fell.

It's weird how you don't think when stuff like that happens. The real world seems distant, far off, rocket after rocket flying overhead, meteors flashing across the inky black of the sky above the city, explosions and fires burning all through the streets.

In the enclosed bubble that was my whole world, I just fell.

I bounced off the ledge and almost yanked my shoulder out of its socket, grabbing onto the edge and dangling from the wall, right beneath the weapons platform as it pounded out another interception.

My ears were ringing.

You didn't want to be up there on that wall a second longer than you had to be. You definitely didn't want to be hanging there, right in the open, easy target for the Imperial troops who had itchy trigger fingers at the best of times.

I hoisted myself back up and crawled out, breaking into a run as soon as I was clear and sprinting along the top of that section of wall, keeping low and taking more care as I ducked under and past the rest of the installations of the defence grid, feeling the heat radiate from them, trying to gauge each time I ran past one if it was going to fire up. My arm was bleeding but I didn't stop.

I stumbled on, running round to the antennae array. I crouched, heart racing, looking down into the flat open expanse of the outer courtyard of the Imperial Garrison.

I should probably explain, the troops occupying our city didn't leave their garrison except to go out on patrol in armoured vehicles or to go relieve the watches at the outposts. They didn't have manned lookouts on that high fortified wall, they relied on their AI. That was all well and good except there was a whole stretch of wall where the stupid AI was blind. It was a hastily-constructed base, sensors break, wires short out, and Kheris wasn't high on anyone's list of priorities. You could dance along that section of wall all night and the AI would have no idea it was compromised. They had thermal and infrared detectors but Kheris was so extreme in its temperatures, they never worked properly. I was fine so long as no one saw me.

That outer courtyard was where they had a running track, shooting ranges, vehicle repair bays. Gunships were landing and taking off at regular intervals. It could get busy but that night it was fairly quiet. I stood, took a couple of steps back and ran, jumping across, grabbing hold of the antennae and using them like monkey bars to swing across and onto the roof of the main complex, the huge octagonal building that surrounded the inner courtyard and the inner sanctum of the garrison that housed the all-important squat little comms centre at its heart. I landed and flattened myself low, crawling to the edge. This was the tricky make or break point. They patrolled that inner courtyard. If someone spotted me, they'd open fire but I'd still have a chance to jump down and make a run for it. Once inside, it wouldn't be so simple to get away if they saw me. That's what was fun. I loved it in there. I loved being invisible, like I didn't exist. A ghost in their military machine.

I waited, watching, then ran round the rooftop, jumping and dropping onto a part of the roof that was a level down. I landed, tucked and rolled, bumping up against the vent I was aiming for and waiting. There were no shots, no yells. No one had seen me. My chest was heaving, blood pounding so hard I could hardly hear and it always made me want to laugh that I'd got away with it. I got my breath back, dug a scrap of cloth out of my pocket and wound it around my arm, biting it to pull the knot tight. It hurt but I'd live. I glanced around, climbed up and slipped into the vent.

It was narrow. It seemed to get more narrow each time I went in there. I shimmied down, scraping my elbows on the rough surface, and braced myself above the intersection. I hooked my feet around a cross beam, hung upside down and looked along the crawl space. They didn't ever bother to install new sensors when they broke. But it never hurt to check. Like I said, I make my own luck.

It was clear. I swung round and crawled into the main conduit. From there, it didn't take much to work my way through into the main outer ring where I could see down into the top floor.

I sat watching for a while. There weren't any sensors or motion detectors in there because the AI wasn't programmed to consider that anyone could be in those spaces.

To be fair, it wasn't that stupid. On the AI gradient, it was about as smart as a ten year old. Its primary functions were pretty routine – heating, lighting, security, monitoring the sensors and auto sentries across the garrison and the dozen or so checkpoints and outposts dotted across the city. Watching every inch of the garrison's main complex wasn't that important to it because no one should have been able to get in. I didn't know anyone else who could get in there. None of the other kids had ever been able to follow me. It wasn't that there was a knack to it. It was just that I could do it and no one else could. It was starting to get tight in a few places, and there was one spot where I had to almost dislocate my shoulder to get through, but I reckoned I had some months yet before I was too big.

I sat there, curled up in that tiny space, and watched the movement down below me through an air vent, timed the comings and goings to check they hadn't changed the patrol patterns, and waited patiently until someone stopped to key an elaborate string of characters into a terminal. That's all I needed.

I waited until it was clear, then dropped down into the room, right into the heart of enemy territory.

It was cool inside. Someone had left a pass on the table. That went into my pocket along with a snack bar I pilfered from a drawer. They had plenty. They wouldn't miss one. I pulled the terminal access point off the desk and sat on the floor with it, out of sight in case anyone wandered past. It took seconds to key in the code I'd just seen, access the main system and instigate a power surge to the main grid. That was simple, just a mass of redirected utility resources with a few neat command strokes. The buildings and crumbling infrastructure of the garrison were built badly enough that it didn't take much to tip it over in spots and I did this often enough with just enough modifications each time that they thought it was a regular glitch. They moaned about it but they didn't suspect anything was awry, putting it down to gremlins.

The lights flickered, failed, and the emergency back up kicked in. It was that easy. I had another trick I did that was even more cool, that's why I needed the pass, but I'll tell you about that later. That night, I didn't need to go too far in, I just needed to grab something valuable enough to sell. I couldn't resist looking deeper into their system though as I saw something that caught my attention. I started to pull up schedules and rosters, and like a fool, I took too long, heard footsteps outside, way too close, and had to hustle to get out, abandoning the terminal and scrambling back up through the vent with seconds to spare as the door opened. I pulled my foot clear as someone walked in, held my breath and eased the ceiling panel back into place.

I didn't have long after that but I knew exactly what I was after. I crawled through, found the workshop I was looking for and dropped down into that strange dim cast of red light.

The drones were all stacked on shelves, a couple spread out on workbenches in bits. I didn't know for sure that none of them were activated, hunter killer drones just sitting there watching, waiting and looking for an enemy to attack. I stood still, staring at them. Nothing moved. There were no blinking lights, no signs they were alive, but that didn't mean a thing, they were designed to be stealthy, invisible, fast as hell. I reached for the workbench, fingers hovering over the array of components lying there, half expecting to get shot at, but still nothing moved.

I wanted to stay longer but there was a noise outside, voices right outside the door. I grabbed a module that was tiny but heavy like it should have been ten times the size it was, and scrambled under the table.

The door opened and I watched combat boots approach, listening as they bitched about the power failing, the weather, the damned dust that was screwing with the sensors they'd spent so long calibrating. The Imperial troops hated Kheris.

They started clattering about with stuff, talking about

where they wanted to be posted next, not Abisko, that was as bad as Kheris, they reckoned, and trying to figure out how to get the damned drone back together when there weren't even enough memory mods there. I was starting to think I could crawl out to the door if I was quiet enough when one of them dropped a screwdriver. It clanged to the floor right next to me as the lights flickered back onto full power.

I made myself as small as possible, squeezing backwards without a sound, as a hand reached down, with more swearing, to grab the screwdriver.

2

My heart could not have beat any faster. I backed away to the other side of the bench, hearing the door open again and more footsteps approach. I moved without thinking, crawled out and half ran, half scrambled for the door, hidden from sight by the workbench and managing to slip through the gap as it closed.

Out in the hallway I could hear voices, distant but getting closer. I ran in the opposite direction, turned a corner and saw a bunch of soldiers up ahead, talking, not looking my way. I ducked back, trapped out in the open. We'd all heard the stories about what they did to prisoners, and that was resistance fighters they caught out in the streets. I'd never heard of anyone being caught inside the base before and I didn't want to be the first to find out what would happen. I looked around fast, running the layout through my head. There were no ventilation panels in the ceiling, no maintenance access in this section of corridor. The voices were getting louder. There was a janitor's cupboard somewhere near. I ran for it, pushed my way inside and clambered into the garbage chute.

It was a vertical drop down, fifty feet at least. I fell, banged my head, curled up tight and bounced. Something jagged in there tore another chunk out of my arm as I tumbled and I clutched the memory module in my pocket, no way was I going to lose my prize.

I hit an intersection and managed to brace myself, legs and arms jammed wide against the walls. There was a hatch just above my head. I edged up to it and fell out into another cupboard. At least two levels down into the base and not where I wanted to be. It was time to split.

It was almost midnight when I got out. There were still a few hours to make it back before curfew ended and the streets started to fill. I climbed out of the vent and made my way back to the fortified wall. I lay there for a moment, flattened against the skyline. Rockets were still screaming overhead, the defence grid pounding out interception after interception. It was only ever the Wintran-made rockets the resistance smuggled in that were that accurate. Most of the time, it was the homemade, cobbled together weapons they used. Those were the ones that did the damage to the rest of the city.

I crawled to the edge and looked over. Outside the garrison wall was a killing ground surrounded by a rubble barrier. The Imperial troops didn't hang out in that open rough area, they stayed inside their walls. They'd bulldozed this part of the city eight years ago when they'd arrived in force to retake the colony and suppress the rebellion, clearing the area for their base, and shoving the remains of our buildings unceremoniously into a twenty foot high barrier that protected them. It encircled the entire complex. The open killing ground was lit up by the sweeping searchlights of the towers all along the wall. There was a trick to getting through it but you had to know the pattern. They changed it and it had a randomiser inbuilt that gave it an extra edge. I'd never had a problem.

I climbed down, careful not to get snagged on the line of barbs and spikes all along that edge. I jumped down, watched the pattern and ran. The rubble barrier was easy, a fair amount of effort but with plenty of handholds and no problem so long as you didn't skewer yourself on the rusting rebar and nails that stuck out all over it. I made it up and over and clambered down to crouch at its base while I sussed out what was happening on Main.

Main Street cut east to west across the city, stretching across in front of me like a no-man's land of broken concrete, dust and grit swirling in the stiff wind that was blowing in from the desert. The brilliant white circles from the searchlights scanned up and down that open drag, glinting off the coils of razor wire blocking each road leading north off it into the civilised half of the city. We lived in the south, the not so nice part of town where you were lucky to find a building with windows intact.

I watched the searchlights as they scanned up and down Main. If you got caught in the light, they had automated sentries that opened up. I followed the pattern until I got it. It was a tough one, randomised with a five sequence alternator and an arbitrary weighter. Nice. I made sure I had it, timed my run and sprinted across and into an alleyway back on our side of the line.

Maisie and Calum were waiting for me on the roof of an abandoned building that overlooked Main. It was our regular lookout point to spy on the garrison.

I made my way up there and dropped down next to them.

"You're bleeding," Maisie said, grabbing my arm and twisting it to see.

Calum punched me in the back. "What happened, squirt?" he said. "You almost get caught?"

Maisie shoved him and whispered, harshly, in his ear. She was older than Calum by two weeks. That made her boss of our gang. And he hated it.

He shrugged her off.

I couldn't help the grin, still buzzing from the adrenaline high. I never got caught and he knew it.

"Don't worry," I said to Maisie, "I didn't leave a mess anywhere."

She rolled her eyes. "That's nasty. Stuff like that gets infected," she said. "You need to go see your grandmother." She didn't ask if I'd got anything. She just held out her hand.

I leaned back and stuck my hand in my pocket, rooting about until my fingers touched the cool metal of the tiny module.

I dropped it into her palm.

She didn't even look at it, just made it vanish with a flourish as if she was performing a magic trick. The money she'd get for it would keep us in supplies for three or four days, five if we were careful.

Maisie looked me in the eye. "Nice one, Luka. Hey, you wanna see? There are new troops. We got fresh meat to torment."

She held out a pair of field glasses. I took them, feeling a shiver spark down my spine, and crawled forward on my stomach to steal a peek over the edge of the rooftop, straining to see the Imperial Garrison, flinching back as the defence grid shot down another rocket that was getting too close and keeping my head low as debris billowed out in a glowing cloud.

The rocket attacks were still fairly regular, sometimes hitting this side of the line, sometimes that, the resistance weren't great with their targeting.

I peeked out again, lifted the glasses to my eyes and froze.

It was him.

3

Maisie nudged me in the leg. "What is it?" she hissed.

From the rooftop, I had a perfect view in through the gate along the main approach into the compound where an armoured personnel carrier was offloading the latest batch of Imperial troops, fresh to Kheris, with no idea what was in store for them.

Except for one. He'd been here before. He was wearing a helmet, stupid not to out there, and goggles, they all wore goggles when they arrived on Kheris, even at night, but I knew it was him. I'd seen his name on the roster in the base but almost hadn't believed that it could be.

Maisie shoved me again. "What's wrong?"

"Nothing," I lied.

I stared across into the base and watched as Charlie reached back into the APC to pull out a kit bag. So he was staying. It had been over a year and he didn't look any different. New stripes on his arm, so he'd been promoted since he was last here but the same laugh as he joked with the guys he was replacing, the same casual ease in the way he moved even though, to him, the gravity was high. Most of the troops posted to Kheris hated it. Charlie never had. We never knew any different. You didn't realise how high the gravity was until you set foot on an Earth-standard orbital or ship. Most of us kids never got off that dirtball to feel it. I almost didn't.

Maisie crawled up next to me and settled on her elbows, taking the field glasses and holding them to her eyes. She looked for a second but it was obvious she didn't recognise him. He was just another uniform. Another enemy soldier to watch out for. "Luka, what's wrong?" she whispered.

"Nothing," I said again.

I nudged her and we shimmied backwards, away from the edge and sat up. I took the thick hooded shirt she held out and shrugged into it, looking up at Calum. "You wanna come in with me next time?" I said, knowing fine well he wouldn't. It was mischief to even ask but I couldn't resist.

He shook his head, looking down his nose at me. "I've got more serious business to take care of."

I grinned.

A rocket hit and detonated somewhere in the darkness behind us, trembling the rooftop under us, showering down debris.

"C'mon, we need to get out of here," Maisie said. "It's not safe." She squeezed my hand and held up the tiny module. "You hungry?"

She didn't need to ask. We were always hungry.

She laughed. "Come on. This should be a good one."

We needed it to be a good one, we hadn't eaten in two days.

She pulled me to my feet and gave Calum a shove. "Race

you back," she said and she ran, dark curls bouncing, disappearing south, back into our half of the city.

I went straight to Latia's place because, although I wouldn't admit it, my arm was throbbing with a heat that felt like it was already trouble. I should explain about Latia. She wasn't really my grandmother, she was actually my great-grandmother, and she lived in a proper house. A real intact home even though it was in the southside. My great-grandmother was charmed and the bombs that had hit the blocks either side of her hadn't made so much as a dent in her walls. She was fairy godmother to all the kids that didn't have a home and she'd given up trying to persuade me to live with her a long time ago. I crashed out there now and then. She still kept my old room for me even though I'd not lived there since she'd got fed up of me running away and finally said, fine, I could go live wherever I wanted. I had a problem staying in one place. I've still never really shaken that off.

That night, she wasn't impressed with me. She made that clear as she cleaned the gash in my arm, splashing precious vodka onto it and binding it tight with a clean bandage. She didn't say a word until she'd finished then she took both of my hands in hers and looked at me intently. "You know what they'll do if they catch you?"

I'd heard it all before and opened my mouth without thinking. "Firing squad. Up against the wall."

She frowned and leaned forward, moving one hand to stroke a finger across the knotted band I wore on my wrist, the one she insisted I wore, for luck, to ward off bad things. It was as if she was reassuring herself it was still there. That I was still protected. She looked into my eyes and whispered, "You are so like your mother, and her mother, it scares me." She stood and turned away. "You know the young ones look up to you?" she said, starting to rummage in cupboards, putting the vodka back into its safe place. "They see what you do and they think they can get away with it too. You will get them killed, Luka, if you don't get yourself killed first."

I chewed on my lip so I couldn't say anything. I didn't want to get into an argument with her. No one ever won an argument with Latia Cole.

There's something else I should let you know about my great-grandmother. She had a daughter, her daughter had a daughter and I was the first boy in generations. It was like it gave me a hold over her, an ace, a get out of jail free card, a pass to do whatever I wanted and I took full advantage every chance I got. I could be a little shit and I knew it. She knew it but I could melt her with a smile. I didn't realise until way later how much it hurt her every time I skipped out. I didn't realise a lot of things. Until it was too late. But isn't that always the way?

Latia turned back to me, hands on hips. "Now make yourself useful and go fetch my box from the cellar."

I loved my great-grandmother's cellar. It was like a peek into another world, almost a kind of museum. She had books, real books with real paper. I used to spend hours down there, trawling through them. Reading everything I could about anything and everything.

She had boxes stacked high, crammed with old stuff, maps, gadgets from another era, clothes no one had worn in decades, mining kit from generations ago when Kheris was first colonised. Everything was labelled, some handwritten scrawls, some printed labels, some in a weird symbolic system code.

There were airtight containers down there she'd told me not to go near. Stuff from the mines and processing plants. I'd cracked one open, years ago, just to see what was in it. There was only this murky liquid that had given off fumes that were in the air before I could snap the lid closed. I hadn't died or anything so dramatic but I'd had a headache so bad I could hardly see for three days and I hadn't been able to tell Latia about it in case she knew what I'd done. I'd left those containers alone since then.

Her box was on a shelf by the bottom step. There was something I needed to do first though so I edged past it and squeezed through into the far corner, ending up on my stomach to crawl under a pile of boxes.

My box was hidden behind a loose wall panel. It didn't take too much jiggling to ease the panel off and drag it out. I sat there, popped it open and as much as I meant to just drop the pass into it and scoot, I couldn't help rifling through all my stuff. This was my cool stuff, the stuff I didn't want anyone else to find. I had a live stun grenade in there, a slick little silver ball that had a corporate ID stamped into it. There were little pots of black and green camouflage paint that Charlie used to give me every time he came back from some other posting where, as he said it, "the whole damned planet hadn't been red dust". He told me once he'd seen oceans that were as big as the deserts on Kheris. That much space, all covered in water? I'd not been able to even imagine it back then. I thought he was kidding me but he'd given me a picture. That was in there somewhere too.

There was also some stuff from my mother but I kept that wrapped up and didn't open it very often. That night, with a bandage wrapped tight around my arm and the gash beneath it still hurting, I reached to pull out that neat little package and, I can remember clear as anything, my hand was almost trembling. Except Latia called down to me and I packed up fast, tucking the pass into the side pocket where I kept them and shoving the box back into its hidey-hole.

Latia took her box with a smile. Getting that from the cellar usually meant lemonade and a good two hours looking through old photographs. This time though, Maisie appeared in the doorway just as we sat down. She ducked past the ragged dust curtain hanging over the doorway and came in. She had a bag in her hand that she placed on the table. Food. But not much of it.

I stood up. "Is that all you got?"

She nodded, scowling.

"It was worth twice that," I said, too blunt, again without thinking.

She knew it but what could we do? She glanced at Latia then pierced me with that look she had. "Dayton wants to see you."

4

I gave Latia a hug, grabbed a bag of chips and ate them on the way. You never kept Dayton waiting. Dayton was KRM, leader of the infamous Kheris Resistance Movement, and if Dayton sent word he wanted to see you, you didn't mess about.

The sun wasn't up yet so I had to be careful, avoiding the patrols as I ran through the city to one of the safe houses. The first one I tried had a cordon around it and a DZ32 tank parked outside. Have you ever seen a DZ? I wish we had a few of those now. Huge, bristling with AG weapons platforms, unbelievable stealth. They could run silent. Totally silent. Except the Earth troops on Kheris used to switch off the suppressors so the noise of them would freak us out. That night, the DZ was stationed on watch, blocking off the whole street, and quiet. It was job done, resistance sympathisers cleared out, and the Imperial soldiers were milling, flashlight beams bouncing, poking about in the buildings nearby. I watched from a distance then split.

I tried the diner next. That was the same. At that one, the soldiers were shouting, on alert, guns up, grunts posted on watch in a perimeter. I shrank back into the shadows of an alleyway across the street. They were emptying the place, marching the staff out in cuffs along with a couple of poor suckers unlucky enough to be in there, and shoving them into stress positions against the wall. Nasty. I could see in the flickering light of the broken neon sign that they were bitching and complaining, but not stupid enough to fight. They'd be questioned then set free. Dayton was careful and he made sure his people were careful too.

I slipped away and headed for the bakery. That was clear. The guy on watch recognised me and let me in.

"They're at the diner," I said.

He nodded. "Yeah, we know." He clipped me playfully round the ear and grinned as he pulled me inside. "Get yourself in there, kid. Don't keep the boss waiting."

There were a few people sitting at tables drinking coffee, talking in low voices that stopped as I walked in. They watched me as I went through, disappearing into the back, past the ovens, breathing in the smell of baking bread and pastries. They sometimes gave us bags of donuts, but nothing was on offer that morning.

I ran down the stairs to the basement and walked in on a card game, smoke spiralling from cigars and a stench of stale beer stinging the air. They ignored me for two rounds then one guy threw in his hand and stood. He gestured me to turn, checking me over and patting me down. I wasn't carrying so much as a pocketknife, never did when I went down there. Although we were all supposed to be on the same side and we were just kids, Dayton was really paranoid about who got close to him.

The guy nodded finally, all without a word, and took me through to another room where there was a hatch in the floor. He pulled it up, gestured for me to go down and let it drop shut behind me.

It was cold down in the tunnels. The kind of damp cold everyone else bitched about but I didn't mind. I don't like being too hot. Maisie always joked that I overheated because I lived at twice the speed of everyone else. It wasn't, it was because we lived on a freaking desert dirtball of a planet. But someone told her once that every living creature gets a finite number of heartbeats. Use them up fast, like a mouse, and you die young. She decided my days were numbered. Someone else told me that I must have nine lives. By then I'd already used up two of them. So I reckoned I was fine for a while yet.

Of course, that was before I joined the guild.

The tunnels snaked under the entire city and out into the desert. The Earth Empire troops occupying the colony knew the KRM had them but they didn't care. It wasn't worth the trouble to clear them out as long as the mining facility was kept running. The only real estate here the Empire cared about was the mine and the space port, and all the defences were geared around those. As far as Earth was concerned, the resistance could have as much of the desert as they wanted.

The tunnels were rat runs, old metro systems abandoned during the war, spreading out in all directions, all the way to the old mines, and rumour had it they were primed to blow at the touch of a button. We didn't believe it, the same way we didn't believe the rumours that some Wintran corporation or another was going to back the rebellion and give us everything we needed to kick the Empire out once and for all. It was all nonsense.

I didn't bother to wait for transport and ran into Dayton's guards about a mile and a half out.

They confronted me as I approached, gesturing with their guns that I had to stop. I held my hands in the air, turning slowly as one of them frisked me again.

I stifled a yawn. They made a big deal of it and finally gave me a shove towards the door.

I pushed through and wandered down the long tunnels, directed at each intersection towards Dayton's command bunker.

No one looked up as I walked in. They were used to me going in there and they ignored me, all of them busy hammering away at terminals or poring over charts.

I stuck my hands in my pockets and slouched by the door, waiting, reading what I could off the screens I could see.

One of the generators must have been struggling because it was fumy as anything in there. I got a headache just standing there.

I didn't recognise Benjie until he sidled up next to me. He looked older. Like one of them now. Like he'd aged way more than the three or four months it had been since he'd left us.

"Hey, squirt," he whispered, pretending to be looking for something in the cupboard next to where I was lurking. Even his voice was different. Deeper.

"Hey."

Benjie had the shadow of a beard. Dark lines around his eyes as he looked over at me.

"I came to check on you all," he said quietly, intently. "You'd moved already."

I nodded. We always moved when our eldest hit fifteen and had to join Dayton. It wasn't so much that we didn't trust them all of a sudden. We just didn't trust anyone who wasn't us.

He knew I wouldn't tell him where we'd gone and he didn't ask. Benjie was the best. He'd taken care of us two years ago, the night the Empire had decided to clear all the street kids out of the southside, and he'd taught me everything I knew back then about keeping quiet and staying hidden. He'd been boss for a long time and he'd been more like a big brother to me for a lot longer. He was the one who'd taken me into the gang all that time ago, when I was seven and getting into trouble, two years after Operation Rainfall when my life had turned upside down.

"How's Maisie doing?" he said.

She only had six months to go before she'd be in here with him. I had a while yet. I was one of the olders, but only just.

"She's fine," I said. She was doing more than fine. But she always had. She'd pretty much looked after us even when Benjie was boss. And everything he'd taught her, she was teaching me.

He smiled then glanced away. Someone was looking at us. He gave me a nudge. "Listen, don't go outside the walls. Stay inside the city. Don't go anywhere near the workshops at the ore processing plant. You hear me? I know what you're like. Stay safe, okay?" And he went back to his work.

Thing is, Benjie did know exactly what I was like. Saying that just made me want to go take a look. And I knew he'd know that. Something was going on and it almost felt like he wanted me to go find out.

I grinned. Benjie was cool. I knew he'd still be watching out for us.

They left me standing there for another half hour. It was weird being in there, watching. Like I was intruding on another world.

Dayton was giving out orders. He wasn't the biggest guy in the room but you could tell he was in charge. He had a way of standing, big shoulders, shaved head, black ink tattoos tracing elaborate designs around his skull, and a tense presence about him that made him stand out even if you didn't know who he was. He'd been running the resistance on Kheris as long as I could remember. Long before that probably. The promise was that we could chase the Imperial bastards off our land and reclaim the riches that should have been ours. Most of the kids bought into it. I just wanted the bombings and rocket attacks to end.

Dayton banged his fist on the table. The guys he was instructing didn't like what he was saying but Dayton shouted the loudest and they sloped out, glaring at me as they pushed past to leave. I sidestepped neatly and watched as he talked quietly to some of the others, a muscle ticking in the side of his jaw as if he was more pissed off than usual, and eventually he looked up at me, squinting.

He raised a finger, beckoning. "Come here, kid."

He pulled out a chair and gestured me to sit. He sat on the edge of the table, leaning forward. He looked more tired than angry. He smiled at me. "When was the last time you kids had anything to eat?"

I shrugged. I'd just eaten a bag of chips.

"They've changed the codes," he said. "Can you get in there and get us the new ones?"

I nodded.

He stood and patted me on the back as he walked away. "Good. You want food? Bring those codes back here, kid, and you earn a week's worth."

Maisie was waiting outside, sitting on a wall opposite the safe house, the rising sun glinting off a couple of intact windows with the promise of a hot day to come. She was shielding her eyes, watching for me, and she grinned as she saw me.

She jumped down and dropped into step alongside me. "What did he want?"

"Codes."

What else would it be? Dayton wanted me, then he wanted codes.

"You didn't get any sleep last night," she said. "You can't go straight back out there."

I didn't stop. "We don't have much choice."

Dayton paid well and she knew it. She grabbed my arm. "Luka, wait."

"I'll be fine," I said. "I'll get you some chocolate."

She pulled me into a hug and shoved me away just as fast.

I grinned and broke into a run. Codes were easy.

5

The prevailing winds had brought in a dust cloud that was hanging heavy over the city as the sun rose and the heat built to its usual stifling intensity. I knew which outpost to go to from the roster I'd seen while I was inside their system in the garrison.

I perched on what was left of the schoolyard wall, dangling my legs and kicking at the rubble.

There were newbies on duty. You could tell because they were still wearing their regulation issue goggles. It took a while for the newbs to adjust to the dust and harsh light of Kheris. I'd heard them bitch about it enough. That and the gravity.

I watched the troops mill around the outpost, weapons out, twitchy as anything, close enough that I could see what was going on, far enough away that they wouldn't tag me as a threat. I was just a bored kid, throwing stones into a bombed out building.

It didn't take that long before an APC pulled up and Charlie got out. He talked briefly with the others then one of them climbed into the vehicle and it left. I waited for Charlie to spot me and jumped down as he waved.

Charlie being there made it easy. I walked forward. One of the newbs brought round his rifle, finger on the trigger, staring at me as I approached as if he thought I could have a bomb hidden under my grubby tee shirt.

Charlie gestured his buddy to stand down and said, "Hey," to me.

"Hey," I said back.

"You've grown. What are you now? Thirteen, fourteen?"

I shrugged. "Something like that."

"Aren't you supposed to be in school?"

"They bombed it."

"The missionary one on the north side," he said. "Aren't you lot supposed to go there now?"

I shrugged again. I'd gone a couple of times. "They didn't like that I knew stuff they didn't." And I'd got into a fight with this huge kid that was picking on the others. Put him in the hospital. They hadn't liked that either.

Charlie looked like he was trying to stifle a grin or trying to decide whether to give me a hard time but then he just said, "You see the meteor shower last night?" He was testing me. Teasing.

I shook my head.

He smiled like he knew fine well that I would have been out after curfew and would have seen it. "C'mon inside."

I followed him into the cool shade of their outpost. He threw me a candy bar and watched as I put it carefully into my pocket.

"What about you?" he said. "When was the last time you ate anything proper?"

I shrugged again.

Standard response.

"Sit down." He pulled out a rickety chair and steered me into it.

I perched there, watching as he dug out a ration pack and put it in front of me. That would cost us fifty to a hundred on a good day. Just that one pack. He rummaged in it and pulled out a pouch of soup, twisting the tab to heat it.

"Don't eat too fast," he said. "You'll make yourself sick."

The newb was staring at me. Charlie glanced at him. "Goulden, go make yourself useful and check on the stat reports." He sat down opposite me. "How's grandma?"

I took a sip of the hot soup and raised my eyes. "She's fine."

"What have you done to your arm?"

There was a small pocket book on the table, open, intricate code filling every line, but it was facing him not me. He flipped it shut as we sat there. It was Goulden's name on the front, not Charlie's. Charlie would never have been so careless.

He gestured again. "Your arm?"

I took another slow sip. "Just caught it on something. It's fine."

Charlie shook his head and stood. "You up for an errand?" He walked round.

I couldn't reach for the code book and open it right in front of him but I didn't need to. I'd seen enough.

"Sure," I said, reaching into the rat pack instead and palming the chocolate bar.

There was a sting on my neck. Cold and sharp enough to make me flinch.

"Antibiotics," Charlie said. "You're welcome to the chocolate. You don't need to steal it." He sat down again. "Do you know the west outpost, quadrant seven?"

I nodded, mouth full of soup.

"I give you a kit bag to deliver and there's more candy." He looked at me seriously. Charlie was always one of the cool ones. He was the one who taught me how to play poker when I was nine. He stuck out his hand. "Do we have a deal?"

It didn't take long to deliver the bag. I took out a couple more ration packs and a med kit that were in there before I dropped it off. Charlie was just playing games, making me feel like I was earning the favours. It almost made me feel bad to steal from him but I was glad he was back.

I headed straight back down into the tunnels. Benjie had gone and Dayton wasn't there but one of the others sat me down. They knew the drill and didn't mess about with any pleasantries. A woman gave me a board and a pen, looking at me like I was a freak when I took the pen in my left hand. I switched it to my right. No one native to Kheris was left-handed. I scribbled out the lines and lines of code, switching it in my head from the upside down glyphs I'd seen in the book, recreating a perfect copy of the cipher currently in use by the occupying Imperial forces.

I was done before anyone noticed. I sat there for a

while, expecting someone to come over and throw me out. When they didn't, I reached carefully for one of the other boards stacked there and sat flicking through it. It was just some kind of manual, tedious as anything, but I'd read it all by the time anyone noticed and came over. They took it off me and said, "Go, scram, get out of here."

That wasn't the way it worked.

"I get paid," I said, standing and squaring up to them.

Everyone else was ignoring me already but one guy said, "Not this time."

"But…"

"But nothing. You want my boot up your ass? Now scram."

I didn't move. He grabbed my shoulder and slapped me round the back of the head hard enough to hurt then shoved me away with a, "Get lost."

It sucked.

As I left, I palmed a couple of gizmos and a screwdriver someone had left on a table on my way out and skedaddled.

Up on the surface, I made my way to the outskirts of the city and the block we were calling home for the minute. High-pitched chatter and squeals were echoing down the street, Maisie trying to be heard, trying to be stern but laughing too much.

They were in the burned out wreck of the old crashed shuttle. It was just a shell, jammed half in, half out of the bombed out rubble of a store front, scavenged for anything useful long ago but cool as anything to play in. I ran up and stuck my head round the cockpit hatch. Maisie was wrestling with two of the little ones in the stripped-out troop section, tickling them mercilessly, both of them screaming. Spacey was sitting in the pilot's seat, on top of the stack of old cushions, playing with the rusted out skeleton of what was left of the control panel. Spacey was one of our littlest. She had an attitude that reminded me of me at that age.

Maisie saw me and eased up, the kids tickling her in retaliation. She fended them off and grinned at me. "Can you remember when we used to play in here?"

We'd seen it crash. I used to pretend I was going fly it out of there.

I grinned back. "When there were still switches in the panel?"

She laughed. "So what did you get?"

I gave the candy bar to Spacey and threw the chocolate to Maisie. "Couple of ration packs."

She frowned. "From Dayton?"

"From the outpost."

She pulled a face and turned back to the kids. "Come on, everyone, we have food. Time to go home." She shooed them out. "What did you get from Dayton?"

"Nothing." I helped Spacey clamber down out of the cockpit.

We watched the little ones run off towards the high-rise block we'd claimed as ours.

Maisie stood in the door, leaning against the mangled frame. "They didn't give you anything?"

"Dayton wasn't there. Benjie wasn't there. Don't worry, we'll get paid next time."

She didn't look convinced. She climbed down and took the ration packs off me. "Whatever you do," she said, "don't let Calum know these are from the outpost."

"It's food. He's not going to turn it down."

She nudged me in the ribs. "That's not what I mean and you know it."

I shrugged. I didn't care what Calum thought of me. I cared about what Maisie thought of me.

She shoved me and grinned. "Is the chocolate from them as well?"

I nodded.

She shrugged then. "I don't care. Chocolate is chocolate."

We chased the little ones home and ran up the stairwell, kicking aside debris, sneakers crunching on broken glass. The whole block had no windows, no heating, no power. No one gave a shit who was in there so it was perfect. It was our hideaway. Our den. Our base of operations. Even Latia didn't know where we were. We were the runaways, the waifs and strays of the city, a steady influx of orphaned kids who couldn't bear life in an Imperial care system that cared more about its image and funding than any children it was landed with. And the constant battles made sure there were always plenty of orphans. Latia took care of us from a distance and that suited us all fine. We made sure she had food and she made us promise that we'd go to her if we needed. It worked. No one bothered her and no one bothered us.

We lived on the top two floors. It was the best place we'd stayed in for ages. It had taken a direct hit from an artillery shell, years ago, and half the top floor had its walls missing.

Maisie headed straight up to the main room, our penthouse suite, and started busying about with the rations. Some of the kids were playing board games on the floor, some of them play fighting in a corner.

Peanut was working at the table. I stopped and emptied out my pockets. He didn't look up. He just mumbled, "Cheers, Luka," and carried on working, peering through a magnifier and working on some piece of kit.

Peanut was our tinkerer. He was eighteen but he was weird so Dayton and the resistance hadn't recruited him. It was their loss. Peanut was weird but brilliant weird. He could fix just about anything. He'd gone and got an unofficial job as a maintenance techie at the space port and he lived there, but he still came back to fix stuff for us. He was the one who'd taught me how to pick an electronic lock and hack into the Imperial command system before I was ten. He'd been caught in the bombings eight years ago and had an arm that stopped in a stump just below his elbow. He had an awesome prosthetic he got from the Imperial missionary hospital but half the time he didn't use it. He wasn't using it that day but that didn't stop him doing the most intricate work I've ever seen. Anywhere. Even in the guild.

He picked up one of the gizmos, grunted and spotted the screwdriver. "Nice," he said and switched it with the one he'd been using.

I used to spend hours watching Peanut work. He never explained anything except to ramble at times, but he didn't need to, I just liked watching him take stuff apart and put it back together again.

"I fixed the alternators on the bikes," he said without looking up.

"All of them?"

He didn't reply. He tinkered a bit more then pushed across a board. It had stats scrolling across its surface. "An IDC ship landed this morning."

"IDC?"

"Imperial Diplomatic Corps." He laughed. "It's black ops. Look at it. The Empire doesn't even have a diplomatic corps. High end stuff for Kheris. And we've got a courier in for repair. Real nifty. Jump capacity and everything." He glanced up. "You wanna come take a look later?"

Working at the space port meant Peanut had an access pass. I always climbed over the fence. When I wanted to play with ships now, I tagged along and played in real ones. A diplomatic vessel meant we could scavenge the latest news from across the galaxy. That was always cool. And Peanut knew I wanted to go see a jump ship. That was the latest manual he'd scrounged for me. I grinned, said, "Sure," watched a bit longer then left him to it and climbed out onto the open window ledge. I stared at the sky. I was tired but too hyped to chill out yet.

Maisie came out after a while. She nodded back towards the room. "We saved you something to eat."

"You have it," I said. I was guessing she wouldn't have eaten much herself. "I'm fine. They gave me soup."

She looked puzzled.

"At the outpost."

"They like you," she teased. She scrubbed her hand through my hair before I could stop her. "You ever wonder who your father was?"

I shrugged. I didn't care. I knew what she was getting at. Not so much who as which one. There weren't many blond kids with green eyes on Kheris. I stood out a mile which meant I had to work harder to hide.

She laughed. She knew I'd never talk about it. My mother hadn't. Her mother hadn't and if Latia knew, she'd never admitted it. An obvious Earth heritage wasn't something to be proud of. Especially not in my family. Everyone knew but I was tolerated because of what had happened.

We sat quietly then she bumped my shoulder and turned her gaze up to the sky. Bright blue and we couldn't see the stars beyond, but they were all we looked to. "Do you ever think of leaving?"

I managed not to laugh but I couldn't help blurting out, "To go where?"

She shrugged then. "Anywhere. Not here."

No one got to just leave Kheris. Anyone who had family to take care of them, money behind them, might move out of the city to the more remote settlements. There were supposed to be places that were nice. Places with trees and wildlife. But we never heard of anyone who got to leave the planet and go anyplace really civilised. Waifs and strays like us? We had no chance.

"One of them might take you," she said, looking down and over towards the outpost.

I bit back the comment that sprang to mind and just said, "I don't think so. Besides, I wouldn't go. Who'd look after you?"

She glanced sideways at me with a smile beginning to crease her mouth.

I was lying. To her. And to myself. Hiding it by being flippant but it was all I wanted. It was all any of us wanted.

6

She gave me a shove. "Go get some sleep." She looked round. "The rest of you... chores."

There were grumbles, mostly from Calum's little crew along the lines of, how come Luka doesn't have to do chores? It's great being singled out as special, it really is.

"Luka gets to sleep," she said, "because he was up all night so you lot would have food to eat."

That was another reason why I was tolerated. I was useful. I made sure I was useful. If you're different, why not be the best at everything to make sure you were so different, no one could say a word against you. It was a fine line and I pulled it off because I didn't care what they thought of me.

"Freddie," Maisie was saying, "laundry. Calum, garbage. The rest of you, tidy up time. Come on. This place looks like a dump."

It didn't. Maisie kept us straight.

"Luka," she said sternly when I didn't move, "go sleep."

I sloped off.

Calum glowered.

Freddie grinned at me as she grabbed the bag of laundry. I gave her a wink and disappeared off to our bunkroom, mouthing to Maisie, "I'm going…"

Once in there and out of sight, I went straight to the window and watched as Freddie staggered out into the street with the huge bag. Freddie was one of the middlings, the seven to twelve year-olds of our gang. She was nine going on twenty nine, small and cute and twice as stubborn as I could be.

It took me two minutes to climb out, shimmy down the rope we had hanging there and run to catch up with her. I crept up and grabbed the bag as if I was stealing it. She laughed and bumped hips with me as we walked, her black hair swinging in its insane topknot.

"Why do you enjoy pissing Calum off so much?" she said.

"Because it's easy."

"What are you going to do when he's boss?"

"Calum won't ever be boss." Maisie had told me a long time ago that she'd never leave me alone with him, that she'd take him with her when she went, just to protect me from him. I'd told her that wasn't necessary but she'd just laughed and thumped me.

Freddie hooked her arm through mine. "You'll be an awesome boss," she said.

I couldn't think that far ahead but I humoured her anyway. "We'll have chocolate for breakfast every day."

She laughed.

It was funny until we saw that the road we needed to go down was blocked off. We heard the DZ before we saw it. It was battered and dirty, its main turret swinging to track us as we approached. A soldier walked round, looking paranoid and hot. He was holding his rifle like he wanted to have someone to shoot at.

He waved us away, saying loud and clear in his brash Earth accent, "Bomb. Take another goddamned route, kids."

It happened every other day. Sometimes they went off, sometimes it was all just drama and inconvenience.

Freddie was craning her neck trying to see what was going on. I steered her away. I had the bag on my shoulder and I swung it round just enough to bump her off balance, surreptitiously picking a candy bar neatly out of her pocket as she nudged me back.

I gave her a smile. "Why are you flunking Math?"

She shook her hair out of her eyes. "Who told you that?"

No one had told me. I'd seen her grades when I'd snuck back into the Imperial missionary school to grab some stuff I'd left behind. "What's the problem?"

"There's no problem," she said, jumping over a fresh crater in the road. "I just don't like the teacher."

"That's no reason to flunk it."

"Says you." She stuck her tongue out at me. "You don't know what it's like. You have it easy."

And there was the lie. They all thought I didn't have to try and they couldn't have been further from the truth. I had to work harder than any of them because not knowing how to do something drives me crazy. It always has. It just looked easy because I made it look easy to wind them all up.

I held out my hand, offering her the candy bar.

Her face lit up. "Thank you," she said then caught herself. "Hey, wait." She glared at me, patting her pockets. "That's mine." She snatched it off me with a fake scowl then laughed and kicked at a stone. "You could teach me algebra," she said, looking back at me all coy.

I nudged her again so she stumbled.

"It's all about balance," I said. "You don't stand a chance."

"You're so funny." She glanced behind us and I got the feeling there was someone watching. She was more solemn as she turned back to me and dropped into step beside me. "Seriously, Luka, you need to be careful around Calum."

I should have listened to her. Maybe if I had, I wouldn't have ended up in the mess I did.

It was that night that the ship crashed out in the desert. We shouldn't even have been out there but I told Maisie what Benjie had said about the ore plant and she'd agreed that we should go see, reluctantly and only once I'd relented and said I'd catch some sleep.

She thought I was reading more into it than there was. "Benjie uses you," she'd said, unimpressed that Benjie was still influencing the gang even after he'd gone. "Do you realise that, Luka?" I told her she was being stupid. I loved doing the stuff he asked me to do. It was a game. Thing was, I got to be better than he was. Much better. He used to laugh and raise the stakes each time, and what was twisted was that it was that that made me better. Like I said, I learned a lot from Benjie.

We skipped out as soon as it was dark. We left the little ones with Freddie and a couple of the other older middlings watching them. We didn't tell them where we were going.

There were plenty of ways out of the city. It was easy enough to avoid the security cameras and guard posts. We took the dirt bikes, made it to the edge of town and took off into the open.

It was a dry night, a chill wind blowing dust in dancing flurries across the surface of the desert. I rode down a bank and hunkered low, dragging a scarf up over my mouth and nose, grinning at Maisie as she spit and spluttered, and throwing her a rag she could use. Peanut was wearing goggles. He looked insane. Calum was sweating, even in the cold air. I laughed at them and rode on ahead.

There was something about being in that big, wide open space in the cold of night. I went ahead because I wanted to be by myself. It made me feel that the universe was bigger than our fraught little corner of nonsense. I don't know if I even believed it back then. I don't think I did. It was just something to hold on to. To hope there was more. To think things could be better. I had no idea of the price that would be demanded of me to get there.

I skidded down into the ditch surrounding the ore plant and abandoned the bike, crawling on my stomach to peek up over the edge. The towers were belching their usual clouds of green tinged gases, steam pouring from vents and pipes to swirl up into the night sky. It was patrolled by guards, a couple of tanks parked at the entrance.

I waited for the others and we worked our way round, slipping through the fence where it went right next to one of the buildings that had been bombed years ago, where the rubble made it look like there was no way through but there was if you knew.

Calum was looking behind us the whole way, cracking his knuckles. Nervous. I knew what was wrong. He was getting big. And he was stocky to start with. He'd look a fool if he couldn't fit through the gaps any more. I half hoped he wouldn't be able to but he did. With a squeeze.

Inside, we had to avoid the buildings of the main processing plant. They were all watched by automated security systems. They couldn't cover every inch of the outside so we could wander around and play, so long as we watched out for the guards. I ducked under a pipe that was hissing steam. The hairs on the back of my neck were tingling, gut instinct screaming at me to leave, but I wanted to know why Benjie had told me not to go out there. Twisted, I know. Trust me, it's not a good way to be. It never ends well.

I worked my way round to the workshops, past the massive storage tanks where they kept the chemicals for the extraction processes. There was a tang to the air, the kind that sticks at the back of your throat. It was like the crap in those containers in Latia's basement. The chemicals were nasty. We had shelters in town that we had to use whenever there was a major leak of the worst of the gases they produced. I gave the storage tanks a wide berth and kept the scarf pulled up tight over my mouth and nose.

The hangar doors of the main workshop were closed. If we so much as approached the doors, we'd set off the alarm. I had an idea of how I was going to get in but I'd never done it before. I told the others to wait and ran round to the waste outlets where the pipes that were twisting out of the building and across to the processing plant were almost too hot to touch. I climbed up and squeezed through, burning a patch of skin off my elbow and jumping up onto a ledge that gave me a chance to get up onto the roof.

I crawled along to the intake I was looking for and looked down. There was a ventilation fan rotating in a lazy spin. It was the only opening that wasn't protected. I watched the motion of the blades. There was a distinct chance that I could either get jammed stuck in there or cut in half. I climbed down, wedging myself above the blades as they swept round the vent, holding my breath and counting.

I went for it. One of the blades skimmed my shoulder, almost snagged my shirt and nearly took off my hand as I shimmied past and dropped. I bounced down the vent and dropped down into the workshop, scrabbling into cover and listening in case there was anyone in there near enough to have heard.

Nothing.

I gave it another minute to make sure it was all quiet,

checked that my shoulder was intact and crept out into the workshops.

From inside, it was easy to hack into the security system and trash it enough to fool it into ignoring us. I set up a feedback loop. They wouldn't even know it wasn't working.

I made sure there was no one in there, went to the front and opened a side door for the others.

I didn't wait for them. It was weird walking around in there, amongst the huge machines, only occasional lights that cast a dim, eerie glow. I wandered around, gawping at the crates. I followed the main aisle and climbed up onto the gantry, getting deeper and deeper into the shed.

It was like having my own private playground.

I walked out onto an overhead beam and waved down at the others as they appeared below.

Maisie yelled up to me to be careful but that just made me climb higher. I ran out along an open gantry and saw what Benjie must have been hinting at.

I dropped down and yelled, "Hey, Peanut, come take a look at this."

Peanut whistled when he saw it.

Calum was struggling to breathe, he was so out of shape. He pushed past us and grumbled, "What the hell is it?"

Peanut was hypnotised by it all and walked forward, almost stroking his hand along the crates and barrels. In the centre of it all was some kind of robot, half built, components glistening in the dim light, towering almost to the ceiling of the shed. It looked like it was sleeping, like it could power up at any second, turn and confront us for trespassing. The rest of its modules and parts were strewn on the floor, half in and out of boxes.

Peanut turned to look at us, goggles perched on top of his head pushing his hair out at all angles. He grinned like a kid in a toyshop, wandered back and whispered, loud and theatrical, "Holy shit."

We left, and riding our dirt bikes back across the desert, it felt like we'd imagined it. Maisie yelled at me, "Was that even real?"

We laughed. Peanut said it was a mining robot but I argued it could be a super soldier. It had an AI, that was obvious from the conduits. Maybe its weapons were in another box. He'd said no way but he'd looked anyway, pocketing as many gizmos as he could without risking anyone noticing too much, and we'd run when we heard the main hangar doors start to open.

We should have gone straight back into the city but Calum cut me up, skidding to a halt and forcing me to stop. He pointed. The old midway telecoms tower was looming in the dust.

"Bet you can't reach the top of the mast," he said.

I'd climbed a few of the towers before but never that one. It was decrepit as hell, abandoned for years and near to collapse.

"Bet I can," I said without thinking and took off for it.

I was half way up, reaching for one of the cross struts and only holding on with one hand, when there was a roar and a tremble in the air that washed right over us. The ship hit the ground out near the foothills, wiping out one of the mining facilities out there.

The fireball was massive. The mast shook, I grabbed for the bar and I almost lost it completely as my hand slipped on the slender shaft and I dangled there, mouth open, staring at the smoke and flames.

The others down below me were yelling. I wrapped my legs around the mast, slid back down and dropped onto the roof.

"They've shot down one of our drop ships," Maisie said.

She was standing right on the edge and squinting out into the darkness. Dayton and his resistance army didn't have many ships but they had a couple of low orbiters that dropped supplies to them out in the desert.

"Not a drop ship," I said.

She looked at me, raising her eyebrows.

"Too much fuel burning." I'd done the calcs from the distance and the height of the thick black column of billowing smoke. "It's a deep spacer." Only jump ships carried stuff that burned like that.

She didn't question me. No one ever asked me how I knew all the weird things I did.

Calum swore. "We should go back," he said.

I stared out into the night as lights began to trail out from the northern part of the city towards the crash site, emergency response and rescue teams probably, APCs bouncing along the dirt tracks, gunships tracking them, scanning the beams of their searchlights all around, looking for insurgents.

"We should go see what's going on," I said.

And that's how I got into trouble.

7

I sometimes wonder what would be different if I'd known then what I know now about that crashed ship. We just wanted to see what was happening. See if there was anything to be scavenged.

We jumped back on the bikes and took off across the desert, eventually ditching them when we got close enough. We ran the rest of the way. I was messing around, half running, half tumbling, throwing myself into backflips and somersaults. Maisie started singing marching songs and we all joined in, laughing. We didn't have a care in the world.

That was probably the last time I can remember ever feeling like that.

We shut up when we got close enough to see the cordon they were putting in place around it. Then we got real quiet, real quick. We kept to the low ground and dried out river channels so no one could see us, hunkering down anytime a gunship flew overhead whether it had its searchlights on or not. We dropped into a ditch and crawled as close as we dared.

"Why would they build a perimeter like that?" Maisie whispered.

It was a defensive ring of overlapping fields of fire, way

out from the crash site, alternate auto sentry positions and manned guard posts.

"Is that to keep us out?" Peanut muttered, "or to keep something in?"

He was paranoid as anything, did I say that?

We sat there in the dust, peering out of our little foxhole. We could just about make out the hulking shape of the wreck in there, plumes of dense smoke still billowing out from whatever in there was burning, debris and wreckage scattered on the desert floor lit up by the searchlights scanning out from the perimeter around it.

The refinery was trashed, mangled pipelines spewing steam, twisted gantries crashed into the low buildings on ground level.

It was eerily quiet.

"Is it Wintran?" Calum said, too loud.

Maisie elbowed him in the ribs.

"It can't be Earth," Peanut whispered. "No way. The guns would be pointing outwards if they were defending it. They're containing it."

Whatever it was.

Calum turned to me. "Go on then, squirt. You reckon you can get up close to it?" He laughed. "Not so cocky now, are you?"

I wish I could say I'd learned something of self-restraint in those happy times on Kheris but you know me, and you know I never have. Even now.

I braced myself to get up, and turned to Maisie and Peanut. "If it's Wintran, it'll have insignia." Back then, there'd been five of the big original mega-corporations still operational. It was too big to be Zang or Marathon and I didn't think it was UM. "What do you reckon?" I said. "Aries or Yarrimer?"

Maisie gave me her look. "Luka, don't."

I threw her a grin. It wasn't every day we had corporate Winter crash-land on our doorstep and upset the Imperial troops so much. She wasn't persuaded but she didn't wrestle me to the ground or anything to stop me going.

I went to climb out and stopped. I could feel it more than hear it. I ducked back down, flattening myself to the ground and gesturing the others to stay low.

They must have emptied half the troops out of the city. A convoy of APCs and jeeps rumbled past, a couple of DZs in there for good measure.

I should have stayed where I was but I didn't. I didn't think, just timed it right, ran out and ran alongside an APC until I could jump and grab onto the side of it.

I hunkered down and clung on, looking back and watching with a grin as Calum tried to do the same. He wasn't fast enough. He never did have the reflexes to act on impulse.

I watched him fume as I left them behind. The problem with bullies is that they don't like to get shown up. The problem with smartass kids like me is that we don't realise when we are showing people up and somehow it always comes as a surprise when people take offence. At least I knew where I was with Calum. He didn't like me and I didn't like him. Maisie was different. Sometimes she'd back me and sometimes she'd back him. And there were times I couldn't tell.

It was a bumpy ride but I held on. I was a lot stronger than I looked, one thing to thank the gravity for.

They drove right up to the perimeter. I dropped down as they pulled up and hid underneath, watching as the back ramp clanged open, kicking up a cloud of dust, boots thundering down. There were fast and sharp exchanges of orders, crisp military precision as they hustled into position. I've never got the hang of taking orders and even then I found it bizarre that guys who were so smart could snap to at a yell from some idiot in command. Charlie had tried to explain it to me when I was nine, the night he was with the gunship crew that caught me out after curfew when they were grounded because of a thunderstorm. Games, he'd said as he was dragging me in out of the rain so I didn't get caught by another patrol. You play the games and you choose which games you want to play and how you want to play them. That was the trick. That was how to be really smart. Then they'd got out the beers and taught me how to play poker.

That night at the crash site, I crouched there in the darkness under the APC, listening, needing to concentrate to understand some of the accents, but getting the gist of it clear enough. Scary stuff. It just made me want to get closer.

I waited until they were getting ready to make their move then scrambled out from under the APC and ran behind the guard post. The next few minutes were a blur of frenzied activity, units getting into place as they prepared to approach the crashed vessel. Something had happened to the rescue teams they'd sent. No one knew what the ship was. And all comms were being jammed. I heard that clearly enough. They were using runners, hand signals and whistles.

They moved out. I watched as they hustled into position, waited a heartbeat and moved forward, creeping up behind them, keeping to whatever cover I could to keep close. I wanted to see if there was any insignia on the ship. I wanted it to be Aries. I wanted to think that a big corporation as cool as Aries could be interested in our little corner of space. Like, maybe if they were here, there might be a way out.

The hull of the ship was intact, damaged, but intact. But there was no way it was ever going to lift and fight its way out of our gravity. Whoever it was trapped in there, they were gonna have to negotiate their way out, and I wanted to see it.

But as the Imperial troops worked their way forward, guns up, and tension sky high, it started to feel like they weren't the ones on top there. They were hesitant, arguing with each other, freaked out and nowhere near in control.

The metallic tang and cloying smell of burning fuel in the air was making me feel sick. There were bodies on the floor, in that no man's land of open ground around the crashed ship, wreckage strewn everywhere. I followed them as they moved past massive chunks of debris that were hissing steam and got close enough to see the detail on the hull of the ship, black twisted metal, slumped on the desert floor in a way you never wanted to see any vessel. It made me feel cold. There was no insignia to see, no badges or name plates. I started to back off, feeling an unease deep inside that I couldn't have explained to anyone. I didn't want to be there any more. There was no curiosity or temptation to know more, I just suddenly needed to get away.

I was already backing off when the shouts from the Earth troops around me got louder. A deep thrumming noise reverberated from the crashed ship. I turned and ran. Rifle fire opened up all around me, sharp cracks that rattled my ears. The sound coming out of the ship deepened, resonating deep inside my chest. I couldn't move fast enough to get away from it. I skidded in the dirt, lost my footing and fell, scraping my elbow and scrambling to get away. The vibration deepened again. It felt like my skin was on fire. The shouts were turning into screams. The pressure in my ears was getting unbearable. It was like the worst thunderstorm I'd ever been in, times a million. I stumbled, ran and threw myself under the nearest cover I could reach, scraping and burning my arm on the twisted metal as I dived in behind it. There was a flash, heat, pressure, then nothing.

I didn't even know what had happened until someone grabbed my wrist. A weight was lifted off me. I blinked.

"We got a live one," someone was yelling, foggy like

they were miles away or shouting through a muffler. There was cursing. "It's just a kid."

They pulled me out. I hurt everywhere and I had to squeeze my hands tight, fingernails raking into my palms, to stop myself from crying out. I could see lights around me but they were swirling in mad spirals so I shut my eyes and tried to pretend it wasn't happening. The voices had Earth accents so I gave in to them, no choice but to trust them, more scared about what Latia was going to say.

They lifted me and I thought I was going to throw up but everything just whirled around for a minute then someone was holding my hand and saying my name.

Charlie. I thought it was Charlie and I tried to say something but nothing would work. There was a cold sting against my neck followed by a rush of warmth. Inviting but I fought it. Delirious. It felt like I was sinking into soft mud. I didn't want to go. I wanted to know what was happening.

I found out soon enough. Back at the Imperial Garrison.

I can vaguely remember someone arguing that they should take me to the city hospital but Charlie said not and they didn't argue with him. I blinked open my eyes in a medical bay. Charlie was standing there with his arms folded.

He said, "Hey," as he saw I was awake, not impressed and not hiding it.

I wanted to ask about the others but I didn't want to let on that they'd been out there as well so I kept my mouth shut, except to mumble, "Hey," back at him. Our game.

I tried to sit up but my head went spinning off and it felt like my eyeballs were going to drop out. Something was in my arm, a line snaking out to a pouch that hung overhead.

"What were you doing out there?" he said.

It wasn't comfortable to talk but I managed to say, "Wanted to see what was going on."

"Did you see anything?"

"No."

Charlie shook his head as if he was really pissed at me. That hurt more than the headache. "You're good to go as soon as you feel okay," he said.

"I'm fine."

"You're not," he said. "Get some sleep." And he turned, muttering something I didn't catch as he left.

I didn't mean to sleep but I must have because it was dark when I opened my eyes again. There was a medic there, checking something or other. She was stressed out, I could tell that.

I sat up, trailing wires, the line in my arm catching with a tug. My head was pounding but the room didn't spin. That was something. "What happened?" I said quietly.

She turned, looked down her nose at me and said, "That's classified, kid. Now lie down, close your eyes and go back to sleep. You understand what curfew means, right? Or do you want me to read it out to you?"

I stared at her for a second, weighed up my chances and lay back down, watching as she injected drugs into the pouch that was dripping fluid into me. Something really bad had happened and I had a feeling I was lucky to be alive.

As it happened, it was worse than that.

8

They let me go the next morning. Maisie was waiting for me, hovering at the corner. She took my hand without a word as I walked up, just walking next to me as we walked away from the garrison.

My eyes were hurting. I narrowed them to a squint and stared at the ground, counting each step and each block until we got home. Two of the others were on watch duty. They stood and stared as we walked up. She nodded to them as they let us pass and she steered me inside. I couldn't manage the stairs so she grabbed me a blanket and we sat on a mattress in a corner, huddled together, on the ground floor.

"Do you know what happened?" I asked eventually.

She shook her head. "We just saw the blast." She shivered. "They're saying it must be Aries to have stuff like that."

I didn't shake my head because it was hurting too much but I muttered, "They don't know what it is."

I'd woken up a couple of times in the night when there were people in the corridor, talking. Harsh, raised voices. People asking why the hell this scrawny kid was the only one they'd pulled out of there alive. They had no idea how I could have survived it when no one else had, except someone said I'd been found under wreckage from the crash. Ten metres from the nearest body, someone said, as if there'd been a calculated radius to the effects of whatever weapon it had been. I must have been just outside its range.

I'd lain there in the dark, listening to them hustle and yell, waiting for the next shot of painkillers. I wasn't scared. It wasn't as bad as the night we got bombed when I was five. Nothing could ever be that bad. I've not been scared of anything since that night.

At one point, someone had shouted out orders to get all the defunct auto sentries out of storage… anything, everything they had, to make a new perimeter further out. They'd been blindsided and they were furious. The language I'd heard would have made Maisie blush.

She twisted round and looked at me intently. "We thought you…"

I thought she was going to cry but she didn't. She pulled herself together. She leaned in, kissed me on the cheek and whispered, "Nice bruises there, panda boy," then she grinned, got up and threw the blanket back over me.

"Where's Latia?" I said as she walked out, trying to stop my eyes closing, eyelids feeling like lead weights.

"Trust me," she called back, "you don't want to see Latia right now."

My great-grandmother was sitting next to me when I opened my eyes. I must have fallen asleep because it was dark outside, different kids on the door.

She had hold of my hand, tight, her thin parchment fingers stroking gently along mine, reaching every now and then to touch the knotted band around my wrist.

I sat up, aches pulling at every muscle in my entire body.

"I'm fine," I said.

"You're lucky." There wasn't much sympathy in her voice.

It wasn't often that Latia came out to our hidey holes. Someone must have gone to get her.

We sat there and I ended up with her arm around me, snuggled into her side, like I hadn't since I was tiny.

I almost fell asleep again except there were loud voices outside, shouts, someone banging on the door.

Latia stood, gesturing me to stay put, Maisie flying down the stairs and both of them reaching the door at the same time.

"No," Maisie said to whoever was out there. "Whatever you want, it's no."

I watched as she planted herself there, next to Latia.

One of them tried to push past. "Where's the blond kid?"

I got to my feet carefully, my body feeling like it didn't belong to me, nausea swirling as my head threatened to spin away. It was the first time I'd ever had a really bad concussion and the worst thing was not knowing if it would ever go away. It felt like never.

"Whatever it is," Latia was saying, calm and firm, "it can wait."

That didn't go down well. I'd never before seen them

react to her the way they did that night. The voice got low and threatening. "Dayton wants to know what's going on and that kid was there. Where is he?"

Other kids were running down the stairs by then. They got between me and the door, some of them turning and grinning.

It was exciting for them.

But then there was pushing. Shouting.

I heard Maisie protest, heard her cry out. The little ones started to scream. The high pitched squealing was driving knives into my head. I wanted to curl up in a ball on the floor. But I didn't want anyone to get hurt. I walked forward instead and managed to say loud enough, "I'm here."

One of Dayton's thugs had Maisie by the scruff of the neck. They shoved her away and backed off. Everyone shut up then, glancing back at me like I was mad. Calum was standing on the stairs, up a couple of steps, watching.

Latia stepped aside, shaking her head slightly.

"I didn't see anything," I said.

"Yeah," one of them grumbled, "I'm sure you didn't. Dayton will be the judge of that."

They beckoned me forward, pulling out guns to make sure no one else tried anything.

My great-grandmother wasn't going to take that. "Really?" she said, holding up her hand to make me stop. "Guns? Here? In a room full of children?"

They weren't going to back down but they glanced at each other and it was one of the others who said, more respectful, "I'm sorry, Ms Cole, but Mr Dayton wants to talk to the boy. He needs to come with us."

She was determined but there wasn't much she could do. "There is no need for the guns, gentlemen."

They looked at me, made a show of putting the weapons away and beckoned again.

I had no choice. I walked forward, feeling the stares on the back of my neck. They grabbed my arm and marched me out.

They kept to the dark streets and even then they were paranoid and kept to the deepest shadows. I could see headlights moving through the city, the Earth military still mobilising, on high alert as if what had happened could trigger the KRM into making a move to take back their territory.

Maybe that's what Dayton had in mind.

I kept my head down and tried to keep up with them, the impact of each footstep sending spikes of pain shooting through my head.

I was fairly sure that Maisie would be following us but I didn't look behind in case I gave her away. Dayton's guys were thugs but they weren't stupid.

By the time we got down to the tunnels and through to the command bunker, I could hardly see. I sat where they told me to and tried not to throw up.

Dayton wasn't there but the rest of them were buzzing, hyped that the Imperial forces had lost so many in one swoop. I tried to shut it all out but every time I started to doze off, someone would shake me awake or slap the back of my head.

I could feel Benjie watching me from across the room. He brought me a drink over eventually and asked if I was okay.

I wasn't but I didn't say anything.

He pulled out a chair and sat opposite me, leaning forward. "What is it? Concussion?" He looked like he hadn't slept in three days.

"Something like that," I said.

"What happened?"

"I don't know. I didn't see anything."

"Didn't I tell you not to go outside the city? You were out there messing about at the processing plant, weren't you?"

I just stared at him. I was still feeling flaky as hell.

"Did you get in?" he whispered.

"Yeah."

He shook his head with a laugh. "I knew you could." He looked up as Dayton walked in. "Just watch yourself, Luka."

I took a sip of the water.

Benjie gave my shoulder a squeeze and sloped off back to whatever he'd been doing.

The atmosphere in the room changed as Dayton entered. Subtle. But there was an undercurrent of uncertainty suddenly, as if everyone was on edge, waiting to see what he'd do.

He checked some stuff spread out on the central table

then he looked over at me. Right at me and said something I couldn't hear.

Someone grabbed my arm, pulled me to my feet and pushed me towards him.

They were all watching.

Dayton didn't even speak to me, just stood there looking down at me.

It was one of the other guys, an older man, who said, "What's going on out there?"

Meaning at the crash site, with the Earth forces, with whoever it was in that ship. They were assuming it was Wintran, I picked up that much. It felt like the entire future of the rebellion rested on what I said next.

I stared back at them. They'd just threatened my family and I had a splitting headache. I opened my mouth to say maybe it was aliens but I could almost feel Benjie willing me not to be an idiot, almost hear Maisie saying don't be a smartass.

"What is it?" someone else said.

"I don't know. I didn't see anything," I said. I could still hear an echo in my ears as if my brain hadn't finished rattling.

Dayton stared back like he was having to stay his temper. "You were with the Earth forces," he said finally, with forced patience. "You were taken into the garrison. What are they planning?"

Comms were down. He had no way of snooping so he was relying on a thirteen year old kid to tell him what was going on. He must have hated that.

I was slouching, not feeling great and not bothering to impress. "I don't know."

He glanced to the side and a door opened. Maisie was pushed through, protesting, trying to shrug off the guys to either side who had hold of her arms.

Benjie stood up.

I straightened up.

Dayton turned away from me and regarded Maisie as she was brought before him.

"Welcome to the resistance," he said.

She started to argue but he got in first.

"You're a very impressive young lady. Understand this – the situation has changed. The rules have changed. What happened last night is just the start. We need all hands on deck. You'll be a great asset to us." He turned away. "Take her for orientation."

I started to step forward but someone grabbed my shoulders, fingers digging deep.

Maisie looked right at me, jaw set, staring right into my eyes as if she was trying to tell me not to do anything stupid. She didn't fight them as they led her away.

Dayton looked back at me. "Now. You don't know what they're planning?" He leaned down and almost whispered to me. "Go find out." He narrowed his eyes. "What we do here is dangerous. You want me to make sure she's safe? You do as I say. Now listen…"

I bit my tongue.

I wanted to argue that she wasn't old enough but I wasn't stupid. He could do what he wanted. They had the guns. They could do whatever they wanted. And like he said, everything had changed.

They gave me provisions and medical supplies as if that made it all okay, but somehow that made it worse.

Calum was waiting outside, loitering there just out of sight.

I walked past him without even acknowledging that he was there.

He caught up to me, scowling. "What do they want?"

I didn't stop.

He grabbed my arm and pulled me round. "What do they want you to do?"

I shrugged him off. He moved faster than I could think right then and he pushed me, hard, before I could duck out of the way.

"Where's Maisie?" he said, aggressive like he thought it was my fault.

I kept on my feet, just about, and squinted at him. It was difficult in the half light of the alley to make out what mood he was really in, if he was worried about her or if he was glad she was gone. I could guess.

"Where do you think?" I said, harsh, not bothering to give him the respect our eldest usually commanded. I'd never respected him before, I wasn't about to start then.

I could almost see the realisation click inside his brain. His stance changed as he thought through the implications. He squared up to me. Mister Big all of a sudden. "So what do they want you to do?"

There was no harm telling him. He was hardly going to rat me out to the Earth forces. "Break into the comms centre."

He stared at me for a second then laughed as if he didn't believe it. Then he laughed harder when he realised I wasn't kidding. "Don't be stupid. That's suicide. There's no way even you can do that."

I walked off but I spun on my heels so I was walking backwards and stared him in the eye. "I can. I've done it before."

9

He stared at me, open-mouthed, no doubt trying to think of a smartass comment and failing. I spun again and broke into a run, leaving him behind easily.

I went straight to the others. I didn't go further than the entrance. I threw down the bag of stuff they'd given me, said to the kids on watch, "Maisie's with them. Calum's in charge. Tell everyone we need to move," and I turned to leave. I reckoned Latia would be in there still, taking care of the little ones. I didn't want to see her and I didn't want to be there when Calum turned up.

No one stopped me.

I went to Latia's place, grabbed the pass I'd stashed there, and for some reason I dropped the tiny stun grenade into my pocket too. Then I went from guard post to guard post until I found Charlie. I waited outside until he came out on his own. I stood there in the shadows, swaying slightly because my balance was still shot.

He looked at me like he didn't believe what he was seeing then he called out, "Luka, what the hell are you doing? Come in here. You okay?"

I almost bolted.

But I looked at him, wanting more than he could ever give me, and I said, "No."

He took me inside and sat me down. They were still on high alert and I heard them muttering that they'd have their asses chewed out for having me in there, but he told the others to shut up and clear out.

He looked at me, shook his head and pulled two beers from a fridge in the corner. He popped them open, sat and pushed one of the bottles across the table to me.

"Do you need a medic?" he said.

I shook my head.

"What's going on?"

I took a sip of the beer. It was cold. Bitter. I would rather have had a soda but it seemed churlish to complain.

I didn't know what to say. I couldn't exactly fess up that my best friend had been taken by the resistance movement they were fighting to force me to spy on them.

Not when I'd been doing that all along.

Charlie narrowed his eyes. "Did the medics check you out properly before they let you go?"

I shrugged and took another sip of the beer, straight from the bottle the way Charlie did. It was pretty disgusting and it didn't get any better the more you drank of it.

He leaned forward and put a hand to my forehead, steadied my face for a second, looking into my eyes until I blinked, and seemed satisfied I wasn't about to keel over.

"What's going on?" he said again.

Charlie had been there. That night eight years ago.

"Is everyone okay?" he said, trying to get me to say something.

It felt like I'd forgotten how to speak out loud.

I put my elbows on the table and rested my chin down. I wasn't safe there. But then I wasn't safe anywhere. None of us were.

"You want to sleep?" Charlie said.

I shook my head.

"C'mon, Luka, buddy, talk to me. You turn up here in the middle of the night… Jesus, I'm gonna get busted back to private if they find you here. What's going on?"

I shook my head again, hardly moving.

He looked at me, took a swig of beer and reached into his pocket. He took out a pack of cards.

I sat up.

He placed it between us.

Memories surfaced of thunder and lightning, the worst storm I'd ever been caught in, being soaked through to the skin and out after curfew.

"You remember how to play?"

I nodded.

He took out the deck, shuffled and dealt.

We must have played for an hour. Mean queen. Game after game. Until he made me laugh by going all in on a bum hand. I knew how bad it was because I'd been tracking the cards. I didn't let on but he laughed and tossed his cards onto the table face up.

He looked up at me. "You gonna tell me now what's wrong?"

I was about to. I swear I was about to spill it all to him. Dayton, Maisie, the codes, all the stuff I'd stolen over the years. Everything. Except someone walked in. Corporal tags on his uniform, a rifle in his arms. He didn't give me so much as a glance. "We've got a problem, Sarge. They want you over in the garrison."

The comms were still down, they were still having rely on runners to carry messages.

Charlie nodded to the guy and stood up, turning back to me and pointing. "Stay here. You can bunk down over there. But I mean it. No skipping out. You understand?" He raked the cards into the pack and pushed it across the table. "Keep them."

And he left.

I should have listened to him but I waited until no one was watching then disappeared, with the deck of cards in my pocket, to follow him.

Usually when I went into the garrison, I just stuck to the main inner complex, sneaking in to the places no one expected anyone to be so they weren't watching too carefully. And since the incident in the desert, the garrison was way too undermanned, on high alert but not enough bodies to take care of the essentials, never mind any internal checks. They were looking outwards, protecting their perimeters.

But the thing with the comms centre right at its heart was that it was secure, isolated, and it was a sealed unit accessed only through an entrance from the central courtyard with a double sealing airlock, bioscans and auto sentries. Only the command level, way below ground, directly underneath the garrison, deep down with the AI core and the power plant, was more secure.

But I hadn't just been bragging when I said I'd been in to the comms centre before. I crouched in the shadows. I had a plan. I watched Charlie flash his pass to the guards and walk through then I took off running.

I ran the gauntlet of the rubble, the killing ground, the wall and the outer courtyard again, jumped onto the roof and dropped into the inner complex. I didn't mess about. I found an empty office, grabbed a terminal and sat under the desk to hack into the system. I was gambling that they wouldn't have changed the access codes. There was no reason why they would have but I still held my breath as I keyed it in.

There was no alarm. No screaming klaxons, no flashing red alerts.

I took my time then and went meticulously through the protocols to reinitiate the pass. It was complicated but it was one of my favourite tricks when I wanted to get deeper in than the top couple of floors. The pass would be a duplicate. They always cancelled a pass if it was lost and issued a new one with a new code. But I knew how to make it look like an administrative error, two passes active to a single ID at once and an order for immediate recall of the second. Whoever it belonged to would be pissed and inconvenienced as well as fined. That was half the fun. I always left the first, original, pass somewhere it could be found. Mind games.

I instigated another of my little power surges to the main grid and had a poke about before I signed out. I couldn't see anything in there about why comms were down. They were running diagnostics constantly. I read what I could and wrapped up, taking a quick glance at the schematics before I left just to make sure I knew what was what, in case they'd changed anything. It just took a second.

After that, I pulled out, put the terminal into my pocket and headed off into the base.

Knowing what to do and where to go was one thing, doing it was something else. The only route I'd ever figured out into the comms centre was down through the complex and into the substructure of the garrison, climbing into the twisted conduits for the cables, wires, vents and pipes that carried everything needed for life support and comms. It couldn't be completely isolated otherwise it wouldn't have been able to function but its security relied on the fact that the substructure was too small for anyone to infiltrate.

Like I said already, I can get into places no one else can. I can squeeze through gaps that would give mice trouble. I'm not claustrophobic. That helps. I'm more flexible than anyone I know. And I'm strong for my build. That's what growing up on Kheris did for a body that, genetically, was not supposed to be there. All that added up to the fact that I could make my way through pretty much any cramped and crowded space, twisting and contorting.

I crawled through to the main manifold where all the kit split up to go where it needed to go. There used to be a spot where the AI watched. But I'd disabled that years ago and no one had fixed it. The only problem could be electrobes, those tiny organisms that were the by-product of AI activity. Did I tell you how much I hate AIs? On a bad day, if the AI conduits were leaking that badly, I'd given up and climbed out, rather than risk suffocating with the damn things. They could be nasty but I was lucky that night and the concentration of them was light enough to be irritating but not bad enough to hurt.

I worked my way through, climbed up and slid into position to watch, right at the heart of the garrison.

It didn't take long to hook the terminal into the system and listen in as the techs processed intel and ran their stuff. They didn't know what it was out there in the desert and it was freaking them all out. It was hard to stay impassive, listening in to them panic, seeing the flaws in everything they were considering and in amongst it all, there was a dreadful unease that nothing would ever be the same again.

I got what I needed for Dayton, left the terminal and the pass in a random office and made my way out of the complex. I didn't hang around. They'd got the power back up so I just split and made for the roof.

Just in time.

The sun was rising by the time I made it out to the wall. I jumped down, sprinted across the killing ground and clambered over the rubble. I ran across Main, and that's when I made a mistake I still think about now. There was something that made the back of my neck bristle. I stopped and looked back.

Charlie was at the gate and he was staring right at me.

10

I should have run but I couldn't. He didn't say a word, just raised his hand and beckoned.

I walked back across Main as if I was hypnotised. I was expecting him to chew me out but he didn't say a word. He took me by the shoulder and steered me in through the gate, past the guards. That side of the outer courtyard was empty except for a lone gunship that had crew buzzing round it. They didn't even look up as we walked past and into the base.

I'd never been in through the front door before. Charlie kept his hand on my shoulder as we walked, gathering stares, a couple of people muttering as we passed. He took me into the mess hall and sat me at a table.

He said, "Stay there," and went off to the servery. There was no queue. There was hardly anyone in there, two soldiers with plastifoam cups, an officer eating on her own, and the serving staff. I felt exposed, sitting there in the centre of the room, my back to the door, but Charlie didn't take long before he returned with a tray. He took a cup off it and slid the rest across to me.

"When was the last time you had a hot meal?" he said, sitting down opposite.

I shrugged.

I didn't touch the stuff on the tray.

He nudged it. "Eat."

I thought he was going to ask where I'd been, what I'd been doing, but he didn't. He sat there, sipping at his drink while I pushed mashed potato around the plate with a plastic fork, making channels for the gravy to run into. I took a couple of mouthfuls but it didn't feel right, not when I knew Latia didn't have much in and I had no idea where the other kids were or if they had anything.

"I need to go," I said quietly without looking up. I couldn't look him in the eye.

"You need to eat some decent food. I'll get you some to take back to grandma and the others."

He was being too good to me and I didn't deserve it. I half-heartedly stabbed some kind of vegetable that looked too green to be real.

The door opened. I kept my head down but I could see Charlie glance round and curse under his breath.

Footsteps marched right up to our table.

Charlie's chair clattered back and I could feel the tension in his stance as he stood to attention.

The voice was sharp. "Why are there civilians in the base? Current status is Red, Sergeant, if you hadn't noticed. Why is there a child in the base?"

I put the fork down and snuck the candy bar off the tray and into my pocket. I was tempted to slip beneath the table but I reckoned that might not go down too well under the circumstances.

Charlie didn't reply.

I looked up without moving. It was a guy in black fatigues, IDC insignia, two officers a step behind him, all pin sharp and hyper tense. The officers were the usual up-themselves jerks that I avoided. I would have thought they had more important things to do than worry about a grunt sergeant offering scraps of food to a feral kid, even if their all important status was Red.

"Captain," the guy in black said, dripping disdain, "remove this child. The sergeant goes on charges. Good gods, gentlemen, we are virtually on a war footing. Let's remember we are representatives of His Imperial Majesty, even this far out in the godforsaken wilderness."

Someone made a move to grab the back of my shirt. I felt it coming and slipped sideways off the chair, ducking out of the way. Boy, was that a mistake. There was a sound of weapons being drawn and readied across the whole room. Charlie was shouting, someone else was shouting. Another hand grabbed for me and I scrambled away, dodging past uniforms as they tried to tackle me. I pushed past, tripped over someone's foot and went flying into the IDC guy. He struck me, backhanded, across the head. I staggered back, caught my balance and just stopped, letting them get me then, firm hands gripping my shoulders. I stuck my hands in my pockets and slouched, throwing a half grin at Charlie as they spun me round and marched me out.

It was hot outside even though it was early, the bright sun already baking the streets. I scarpered as soon as they let me go and didn't stop until I was out of sight. I reached into my pocket and pulled out the stuff I'd lifted from the mysterious asshole in black – a credit stick, a packet of gum and some kind of data access key. Not much use to us. But to have lost them would piss him off enough to make up for whatever they did to Charlie. I grinned, stashed it all back in my pocket and ran.

As I made my way back down the tunnels, Dayton's crowd were quieter, more subdued, as if they'd enjoyed the euphoria of their second-hand victory but now they didn't have a clue what to do next to make the most of it.

I was escorted into a tiny room that felt more like a cell and sat at a table. It wasn't the usual routine. They gave me a board and a pen, then left, leaving an armed guard on the door.

I scribbled, half-heartedly, using my left hand because no one was watching and not bothering to keep it neat. I finished and sat, nothing else in there to play with.

It was an age before some guy I'd not seen before came in with more boards. He had a black band around his wrist. I registered it as he placed them on the table because Charlie wore one the same. I didn't know at the time what they were.

"Crack these," he said, "and there'll be food."

"I want to see Maisie."

"Crack these," he said again, slow like I was stupid, "and there'll be food."

He pushed them towards me and walked out.

I ignored them.

Then I got bored and couldn't resist taking a look. They were cool. Puzzles. Codes, but not military codes like I'd always had before. These were complicated. I got the first few easy then it got harder.

I sat up.

I can see patterns and I can remember stuff. I didn't know it then but that was the first time I encountered AI logic strings. It was the first time I'd ever played with anything that really tested me. I forgot eating and drinking. I forgot the nagging headache. I pushed the boards aside as I completed each one, some leading onto more and more complex tasks, some simply lighting up green as I cracked them.

They got harder and harder.

I did the last one and looked up, feeling like someone was watching. The guard was still at the door but he wasn't looking in and there was no one else.

I glanced round. There was nothing obvious that was surveillance but that didn't mean there wasn't any. I pushed the boards away from me and sat there, waiting.

I felt hungry then.

No one appeared.

I got out the pack of cards and started to play, dealing hands as if there were people there, counting the cards and playing games, shuffling the way Charlie had shown me, and messing about.

I ended up dealing every card in the pack as fast as I could, face up into five neat piles, until I had one left in my hand. I knew what it was. I shuffled and did it again. I knew what it was each time. I must have been saying it out loud because someone did come in then. The guy with the wristband. He sat down, grabbed the deck and shuffled then stared at me and said, "Do that again," planting the deck in front of me.

I looked at him. "Do what?"

"Don't be a smartass, kid, just do it again."

I dealt until I had one card left. He beckoned me to give it to him. It was tempting to peek, make him think I'd been cheating the whole time, but he took it before I could.

"What is it?" he said.

"Queen of hearts."

He narrowed his eyes and said again, "What is it?"

I should have given him another wrong answer, then they might have left me alone, but I was an idiot and I couldn't help saying, "Four of diamonds."

"Son of a bitch." He threw the card down face up. "You're counting the cards."

I had no idea what he was talking about and I know now that he was the idiot. I wasn't counting the cards, that was way more complicated, I learned that much later. What I was doing in that little cell was just keeping track of them. I knew exactly which ones had been dealt so I knew what was left. I could see the deck and how it was playing out.

I didn't say anything. I shrugged. "I finished all your puzzles. Do I get to eat now?"

I was close to nodding off when the door opened and Maisie came in, pulled up a chair and sat close. She pushed a packet of biscuits into my hand.

"Have you moved?" she asked, hesitant. She knew what the answer would be but she still asked.

She looked different. Even in just one day, she looked different. She was wearing body armour, hair pulled back into a rough pile on top of her head and a scrim scarf loose around her neck.

I nodded. "Are you okay?"

She gave a half smile. "Don't worry about me."

"What does Dayton want now?"

She shrugged. She hugged me and whispered into my ear. "They're trying to figure out what to do next. They want to make a move but they don't want to screw it up like last time. They think if the Earth forces are spread thin enough, they could take back the mines. They're going to hit the outposts."

She said 'they'.

I grinned. "They let you in on all that?"

She smiled, chin up indignantly. "No, of course not. What did you get?"

"They still don't know who it is out there." My 'they' were the Earth forces. We were stuck between the two and didn't belong to either. "But they've taken it as an act of aggression and they're assuming it's Wintran. They've sent for reinforcements so if Dayton wants to make a move, he's on a deadline."

It was more complicated than that but I didn't elaborate.

I didn't want to give them too much. And as much as this was Maisie, she was with them now.

She squeezed my hand and whispered, "Be careful."

I whispered back, "Always am," and she slipped away and disappeared as Dayton and his cronies walked in.

He sat down opposite and pushed a board across the table. It had a weird pattern on it, swirling characters that shifted as you looked at them. I wasn't sure for a second if it was my eyes. But Dayton looked at me and said, "Solve it."

I almost said, solve what? But as I looked, they started to settle out into lines. I swiped a finger across the surface and nudged a couple. It was too easy. One more nudge and it clicked into place.

I looked up. I half expected him to laugh, say that was just for starters and then get out the next one. I had no idea why he was testing me.

He almost nodded at me but then he just picked up the board, held it out to one of his people and said, dry and cold, "Get this to Yardman. Tell him, he's just been beaten by a ten year old."

He knew fine well I was thirteen.

He gave me another board. "Draw me a map of the garrison."

They had a map. I knew they did. I'd seen it.

"Include all the security positions and AI black spots," he added, and stood, patting me on the back.

I sat there with the pen poised over the board, biting

my lip, stomach cold. It felt like I was betraying Charlie but to refuse would be betraying Maisie, and Latia, and everyone else.

"We don't have all day," someone said.

I couldn't figure out which was worse so I did it. I sketched it all out in immaculate detail, in plan and cross section. I made it the official map, not the classified version I'd seen one time when I'd been snooping deeper than usual. That had secret tunnels, emergency breakouts, a hidden vault most of the personnel in there didn't even know existed. I wasn't about to give Dayton all that. I finished it, drew some tiny little skull and cross bones around the edges, added some arcane-looking symbols, and looked up. The little cell was empty except for one bored-looking woman leaning against the far wall with her arms folded.

"About time," she said. "Now scram. We'll let you know when Dayton wants you again."

It was late afternoon by the time I made it back to the block. They'd all gone. No trace we'd ever been there. I sat on the front steps and was tempted to lie down right there and sleep but I needed to find something to drink. I could feel that I was starting to get flaky.

I rubbed my eyes and looked around. We had a system. You needed to know it to look in the right place and we always changed it whenever one of the olders left. I spotted the chalk mark, adjusted for the current regime and followed the marks, half expecting Calum to have pulled a fast one and left me high and dry, but if he'd tried, someone must have ignored him because they led to a door and Freddie was waiting there, on watch.

There was a rifle propped against the doorframe.

"We thought you'd gone as well," she said, almost breathless.

I gave her a hug, and whispered in her ear, "Never."

She laughed. "Go on through. We're in the basement. You need to take the left tunnel."

We never used the basements. It was too easy to get caught and trapped underground. Calum was a fool.

She rolled her eyes like she knew what I was thinking. "I know," she said. "I know. He wouldn't listen. Go on. Get inside. Get some sleep. You look terrible." She took a packet out of her coat and pushed it into my hand. "I saved this for you. I knew you'd come back."

I muttered a thanks and hesitated. I didn't want to go inside. "What's with the rifle?"

She looked serious then. "Calum's insisting. We've all got them. He said everything's changed. He said the Earth forces are freaking out with that thing in the desert and he wouldn't put it past them to try to clear us out again. He said we need to be able to defend ourselves."

I almost said it was Dayton we needed to defend ourselves against because he was about to launch an offensive and we were going to be stuck in the middle again, but I bit my tongue and said instead, "Where did the guns come from?"

"Calum got them from Dayton."

It made me feel cold. "Where's Latia?"

"Gone home."

I stood there, rooted to the spot, biting my lip.

"Go inside," she said again. "Come on, Luka. Don't make things worse. We need you."

Going to crash out at Latia's seemed more tempting but I let her nudge me inside. It was a mistake. Everything had changed. And it would never be the same again.

11

The basement was musty. I stopped halfway down the steps, nose wrinkling, the damp air catching in my throat. You know I said I'm not claustrophobic? I'm also not stupid. I trust my instincts and I know when a place is bad news.

I started to move back up but someone appeared behind me. One of Calum's cronies.

He laughed and prodded me in the back. "We were wondering when you would show up, squirt."

I turned and squinted up the stairs. It was Bram, not just a crony, it was Calum's brother, younger but bigger. He had a rifle slung on his back and a gun in his hand. He waved it at me as he saw me looking at it.

"Go down the stairs, Luka, before I push you down."

I didn't give him the satisfaction.

"Where's Peanut?" I said. "Is he here?"

"He's busy."

He pushed me again as we reached the bottom. They'd strung lamps up, faltering, flickering points of orange glow. He pushed me ahead of him into the tunnels and grabbed me as we passed a door. "You're in here."

There were a couple of middlings in there.

I almost laughed. "I'm not…"

He pushed the door open. "You are now. Rules have changed. You're a middling."

I stood my ground. "That's bullshit. Where's Calum?"

"Busy."

"I'm not staying down here."

"Get in there, you little Imperial bastard, or you'll be going in with the babies."

I could feel them all looking at me, the middlings, the olders that were coming out to see what was going on.

"Where's Calum?" I said again.

Bram reached to grab my shirt. I ducked aside, fists clenched. He was on me before I could get clear, one arm around my neck, slamming the grip of the gun into my face. I got in a few punches of my own, stamped on his foot and wriggled free. Even when you're smaller than them, there's always a way to win. Benjie had taught me that. He'd taught me how to fight dirty, one of the first in a long line of tricks he'd shown me. Always assume they're trying to kill you, he'd said, never give them an inch and if you can run, run. The main thing is to stay alive. Problem was, down there, there was nowhere to run.

I backed off and got a punch in the back as someone else joined in, shoving me forward. I'd had fights with Calum and his cronies before but there was something different that night. Bram grabbed me and pushed my head down, battering me with the gun.

Everyone was yelling. I could feel blood streaming down my face. I twisted and jabbed my elbow backwards, hard as I could, making him roar.

I tried to get free but another blow to the head from behind made my knees go. Someone kicked me in the back and I went down, spitting blood. I raked up a handful of dust as I hit the floor. I wasn't about to roll over and let them win.

A kick to the head made my vision swim. I got one foot under me, blinked, figured out how many there were and where each one was then turned and threw the dust into Bram's face, dodging aside as another kid stepped in to kick me again. He missed. I scrambled to my feet and shoved him off balance, turning fast to avoid a blow from Bram who was screaming curses at me. I might have laughed. That always made them more mad. If someone's pissing you off, don't get angry, laugh. They hate it.

Bram came at me again but someone grabbed him, pulling him off me.

I thought for a second that was it but someone else caught hold of me, spinning me around and landing a barrage of punches I couldn't duck against the back of my head.

I went down.

There isn't much you can do against that.

They were laughing as they hauled me up and dragged me aside. I was kicking and screaming. Trust me, I was kicking like hell, but they were too strong and there were too many of them.

They threw me in somewhere. I hit the floor and heard the door slam, a heavy bolt sliding home as I went sprawling, not far because it was some kind of damn cupboard. Pitch black and damp. I hit my head against something hard and scrambled to my feet, yelling, "Hey," and hammering on the door.

"New rules," someone yelled back. "Fighting gets you one hour in the sin bin."

They all laughed.

I punched the door again and spun round, feeling my way about, coming up against nothing but empty shelves and bare brick walls. I even climbed up to check the ceiling. There was no way out. I tried the door again then clambered up onto a shelf, wiped the blood out of my eye and tucked my knees up tight. It sucked but there was nothing I could do. I'd learned a long time before that how long I could wait in the dark.

After two or three hours, it felt like longer, there were voices outside, a faint orange glow appearing along the floorline below the door. I was stiffening up in the damp cold. I stretched, muscles complaining, my eye throbbing and the blood on my face and neck dried to a caked-on mess. They were arguing, someone that sounded like one of the middlings saying they should let me out, Calum saying, "No, let the sucker sweat in there. Little bastard broke Bram's nose."

That was something. I had to stop myself laughing.

There were sounds of shoving and scuffling, and more swearing then it was quiet again. The thin glowing line at the bottom of the door dimmed and vanished, leaving me in total darkness again. The thing about fear is if you let it, it consumes you, but face it, give it a neat sidestep and stare it down, then you take away its power. The guild psychs used to tie themselves in knots over me. They analysed us all to pieces. Full profiles on anything possible. According to everything they had me sussed as, they used to say that being locked down in isolation should have been my worst nightmare. I always laughed and said, "Yeah, been there, done that." It wasn't the only thing they called me on. They didn't like me. I'll tell you about that some time.

Back then, when I was thirteen and shut in a dark hole, I sucked it up. They couldn't hurt me any more. Someone would come let me out or they wouldn't. I closed my eyes and breathed slow and steady. I could give it as long as it took.

It didn't take that long. There were muffled shouts outside, excitable, pounding footsteps and yells.

I could hear Calum shouting, the little ones squealing, then clearer someone shouted, "Come on, there's something going on out in the desert."

I sat up.

It went quiet again for a while. I listened to the silence then there was a scraping sound as the bolt was tugged back, with a struggle, and the door opened.

Freddie stood there, looking small, a weird mix of pissed off and dismayed flashing across her face.

I squinted at her. "I'm fine."

She held the door open. "This isn't right. They shouldn't have done this. Not to you, of all people."

I jumped down, trying to be more cocky than I was feeling.

"I'm fine," I said again.

She pulled a face. "You don't look fine." She held out her hand. "Come with me."

She led me to a common room. It was deserted. Messy. Rubbish everywhere. They'd hardly been there five minutes and it was a dump.

Freddie sat me down, shoving aside a pile of dirty clothes.

She disappeared for a second and came back with a wet cloth that she held out to me, muttering an apology. "We didn't know where you were. They only just admitted it. Calum said I could let you out. I'm really sorry."

I pressed it against my eye and gave her a half smile. "It's not your fault. They're idiots. Did I really break Bram's nose?"

She laughed and beckoned for the cloth. "Come here. You're a mess."

I let her dab at my face.

She stared at me intently the whole time. "Is Maisie really gone?" she said finally.

I nodded. "She had no choice."

Freddie sucked in a deep breath. "She'd hate what we are now."

I didn't know what to say. I hated it.

She took my hand and pulled me up. "Come on, you need to see this."

I followed her up onto the roof. I heard it before we even got up there to see. I knew what deep spacers sounded like when they came in to land.

There was a constant low rumble like thunder. It wasn't as good a view as our last place but we could see what was happening. Massive dark shapes were dropping down into the desert. They were bombing the crap out of the crashed ship, surrounding it.

Klaxons were going off all over the city. I could see the Earth troops pulling back, abandoning the loose cordon they'd been guarding.

Peanut was up there.

He looked over. "You okay?"

I shrugged. "What's going on?"

He was holding field glasses. "Winter," he said and handed them to me.

I took a look, heart sinking into my stomach. "It's UM." I recognised the silhouettes of the gunships and drop ships as United Metals even this far off.

Calum and his cronies were whooping and waving their stupid rifles in the air.

I felt sick. The last time the Wintrans were on Kheris in force had been eight years ago when they'd abandoned the KRM rather than risk a direct military confrontation with the Empire.

"This is what we need," Calum yelled and laughed.

He turned and stared at me. "The stinking Earth forces won't know what's going to hit them next." He whooped again and ran off, Bram and their buddies following, fists pumping and hollering.

It wasn't right. That wasn't the way we were supposed to be.

We sat there, watching the sun drop and the full might of the Wintran militia descend on our desert.

"This is not what we need," Peanut said quietly. "What does he think is going to happen? UM will run the Empire off the planet and hand the keys to Dayton? I don't think so."

Freddie climbed up onto the parapet. "UM wouldn't do that to their own, would they?" she said. I already said, didn't I, that she was old beyond her years? Way more switched on than Calum. She glanced back at me. "Didn't you reckon it was Aries?"

I shrugged. Whatever it was, UM must have thought there was something in there worth fighting for.

"Do you think they'll turn on the city?" Freddie had only been two when it had happened. She didn't really remember it but she'd heard enough to be scared.

I couldn't answer.

Peanut stood up. He was rubbing his arm. "Freddie, you're supposed to be on watch," he said, almost distractedly. "Get yourself back to the door and take the others inside with you."

She scowled but she didn't argue.

I drew my legs up and hugged my arms around my knees, resting my chin down and staring out at the onslaught, trying to shut it out and not fall back to that night.

"They won't," Peanut said when it was just us left there on the roof. He looked back down at me. "Luka, listen to me, they won't." He nodded back towards the desert. "They're here for that."

I sucked in a deep breath and stood up. "I'm going to stay with Latia. Calum's an idiot. You want to come with me?"

He nodded. "In the morning. I've got some experiments running but they should be done by then. You want to see?"

Peanut's experiments were always cool.

"I'm trying to crack whatever it is jamming comms," he said. "I thought I had it. I reckon a couple more hours. You get anything juicy from the garrison?"

I stuck my hands in my pockets. I'd forgotten about the stuff I'd grabbed. I held them out to him. He declined the gum but his eyes lit up at the key and the credit stick.

"Nice," he said. "Come on. Screw Calum. We'll be gone in the morning. We'll set up a new gang, you and me. We'll take the little ones. Freddie'll come with us. The rest can decide if they want to stay and play games with the big boys."

Like it could ever have been that easy.

12

I followed Peanut down into a dingy room he'd set up as a workshop. He must have brought a load of kit from the space port. He waved his hand towards a tatty sofa.

"Make yourself at home," he said, settling himself at a table strewn with tools and gizmos. He tossed my latest haul onto the pile and picked up a screwdriver.

I sprawled on the sofa. It was musty as hell but I was about done, ribs aching and a headache pulling at the base of my skull. I pressed the cloth against my eye and stretched out.

"You shouldn't antagonise them," Peanut said as he worked.

"I don't try to." I shifted my weight but couldn't get comfortable. "I don't know why they hate me." That wasn't totally true.

Peanut laughed. "Because you're too good at what you do. And because Maisie likes you. That's why Calum hates you."

My stomach flipped just at the way he said that. It should have been funny but I was too sore to think about it. I couldn't believe I'd let myself be hijacked by brainless thugs like Bram and his cronies.

I flung my arm over my eyes.

"How is she?" Peanut said, more seriously.

"Maisie? She's fine. She won't let them give her any stick. She said they're going to hit the outposts, take back the mines."

He snorted. "It'll be a lot of noise, a lot of alpaca shit and not much else."

I wasn't so sure. "Do you think UM will stay?"

"You mean will they throw in with Dayton and take over the colony? No way. There's nothing here for them. I told you, it's not going to be like it was."

There was a noise at the door.

"Like what was?" Calum said, striding in like he owned the place.

I sat up.

Peanut didn't look up.

I couldn't resist. "Like kindergarten was when we used to fight over who got to play in the sand pit."

Calum didn't look impressed. He swept up a couple of gizmos off the table and kicked my legs as he walked past. "What are you two numbskulls talking about? Like what was?"

"Like it was eight years ago," Peanut said, blunt.

Calum swore and tossed the gizmos back onto the table. "Christ, don't you two ever let up on that?" He pulled a handgun out of the back of his waistband and banged it down in front of Peanut. "This is shit," he said. "It keeps jamming. Quit screwing around with whatever you're messing with and fix it." He shoved it forward and turned on me. "And you…" He pointed at me. I'd never noticed before but he had a tick over his eye. He glowered at me. "Stay away from my brother. You lay another finger on him and I'll break your legs. You hear?"

There are times when you need to jump up and fight your corner and there are times when you just have to shrug off the crap and save it for another day.

My head was aching. I saved it.

He didn't like that I didn't bite and he took a step forward but one of his cronies stuck his head around the door and said, "Calum, Dayton wants to see you."

Calum smirked. "Dayton wants to see me," he said, like that set me in my place. He walked away, tossing in a throwaway, "Get your ass into the middlings' room, Luka," as he walked out.

The door slammed shut behind him.

Peanut swore again and shoved the gun out of his way. "Keeps jamming? All handguns on Kheris jam. What does he expect in this dust?"

I didn't care. I didn't like the guns and I didn't like the dingy basement. My stomach felt cold and it had nothing to do with the pounding I'd taken. "I can't stay here," I said.

"None of us should stay here," Peanut said. "Give me a couple of hours. This won't take long."

I was almost dozing off when Peanut cursed, low and intense like he always did when he had something cool. I opened one eye.

"I knew it," he muttered, hunched low over some kind

of panel, turning dials and working a board. "It's not electronic."

"What isn't?"

"Whatever it is that's blocking out all our comms. It's not electronic. It's coming from that ship out there. It's some kind of energy but it's pulsing like nothing I've ever seen…" He tweaked a control. Sparks flew and the machine screamed. Peanut flinched away, darting his hand in to flick it off. "Jesus."

I pinched the top of my nose, headache spiking. "Does Aries have stuff like that?"

"Never heard of anything like it."

He started muttering to himself, peering at the board and plugging more gadgets into the panel. I wish now I'd taken more notice of what he'd been doing that night. It's not often I ever regret anything. Live for the moment. That's what that night eight years before all that had shown me. Etched into my soul. Live for now. There might not be a tomorrow. But what Peanut had been so close to that night… it could have changed everything. It could have changed the outcome of the war. But as it happened, we never had the chance. People suck and nothing sucks worse than someone thinking the worst of you for no reason other than jealousy or insecurity or whatever the hell it was, and that night, I found out how much it sucked.

I didn't mean to sleep but I must have because I woke to shouting. It was Peanut I could hear protesting, swearing, and as I moved to sit up, rubbing a hand across my face, someone pulled off the blanket Peanut must have thrown over me and grabbed my arm.

One of Calum's buddies.

I shrugged him off and scrambled backwards, hitting my head against the low wall.

There was more shouting. Eventually someone yelled for quiet and everyone seemed to look at me.

I stared back, not sure who was on my side any more.

"Calum wants to see you," someone said sullenly.

It was like being summoned to see Dayton.

I wanted to tell them to go screw themselves and almost grabbed the blanket to pull it back over my head but the way some of the little ones were looking at me, never mind Peanut, made me take a slow intake of breath and say, "Fine, he just needed to ask."

They made way for me. I followed one of them through dark rooms, lanterns flickering in corners, stashes of crates and boxes I'd never seen before. Some were labelled rations, some with numbers that looked like it could have denoted ammunition, most of them anonymous, sealed. They could have been anything. Dayton had never given us that much before. Anything I'd been paid had been scraps, just enough to keep us going back for more. It didn't feel right. As if some deal had been done and it wasn't just that I'd had no part in it that made me feel queasy.

The kid leading the way was wearing a gun in a holster

on his hip. He touched it now and then as if he wanted to reassure himself it was still there. It was ridiculous. We'd never carried weapons. They wouldn't have a clue how to fire straight if they tried. I should have seen then what was going on. And I should have run a mile.

Eventually we came to a door that was being guarded by Calum's best buddy, standing there with a rifle in his arms. I almost laughed. I think I might have done because someone slapped me on the back of the head and they pushed me through the doorway.

Calum was sitting at the far end of a table like he was lording over it in his own private war room.

"Luka," he said.

"You the big boss now, Calum?" I said. "This is all shit. You do know that, don't you?"

He regarded me as if he was pondering some immense decision.

"Your soldier buddy is looking for you," he said, finally. Derisive. "He's leaving messages everywhere. He wants to see you."

"Why?"

"Why the hell should I know? You'd best get out there and see what they want."

I stared back at him.

"West outpost," he said. "Get your ass out there. See what the Earth boys want. Now scram."

He said it the same way Dayton's guys said it and he laughed.

I walked out, my skin crawling.

I'm sure you know this, but as much as being smart is cool, it makes dumb people scared of you and petty people paranoid. My problem was, I couldn't hide it. I couldn't help speaking out or doing stuff. From as early as I could remember, Latia always warned me against showing off and I swear, it was never that. I couldn't help it. I loved doing things when I didn't know if I could or not. It was always a higher wall, a tougher climb, a more insane jump, a trickier lock. The other kids didn't get it. They got scared and ran from what made them afraid. I ran to it. Headlong. Because that's the only way I had to keep the nightmares at bay. If that's what made Calum hate me, fine, I wasn't going to change. I just needed to get away.

Calum and his crowd shouted stuff to my back but I didn't stop. I kept walking and worked my way out. I went and found Peanut, sidled up close and slipped the knotted bracelet off my wrist. "If I'm not back in three hours," I said quietly, "take this to Latia and tell her I'm sorry." She'd know I'd never take it off unless something was wrong. I just had a bad feeling about all this.

He looked at me horrified, like he wanted to argue, but he was also looking slightly behind me, over my shoulder, and I could tell Calum or one of his buddies was there.

"It's fine," I muttered and I left.

I could hear the rumblings of thunder in the clouds, rolling in from the foothills, and there were spots of rain in the air. It wasn't quite dark. That crappy time between daytime and night when the light was weird and shift change meant the guards were all hyper-alert waiting for curfew to kick in. There weren't many people about, even in the main streets as I worked my way over to the west side. A few scurried past, trying to get indoors before the storm broke.

The outpost over in the west quadrant was right next to an area that had got the crap bombed out of it. No one had ever bothered to rebuild or clear out the ruined buildings.

There was no sign of Charlie. I clambered up onto one of the rooftops, lying down on my stomach under an overhang of mangled corrugated sheeting, getting the position right so I could see everyone coming and going. Then I waited.

It started to get dark after a while. The searchlights on the roof of the outpost arced into life, white beams cutting through the inky blue black of the night. There were no other lights in that quarter of the city. From my vantage point, I could see right out into the desert to where the hulking shape of the crashed ship lay surrounded by a cordon of UM forces that were still pounding it.

Different vehicles drove up to the outpost a couple of times but still no Charlie.

The wind was picking up, swirling vortices dancing out on the plain and gusts starting to send heavier and heavier flurries of rain into my little shelter, turning into an insistent pounding on the sheeting over my head. And it was getting cold. I wasn't wearing much and as I got colder and it got darker, storm clouds gathering, it was tempting to jump down and go find out what was going on. Except none of the other soldiers would take as light a view as Charlie did to a kid being out after curfew.

I was starting to think something must have happened. I shifted my weight and hugged my arms around myself to keep warm. Time to bug out. I wasn't stupid.

Turns out I was.

I climbed down into an alleyway and dropped down, a scuffing sound of feet on the rubble behind me, and a ringing of metal on metal.

I turned, saw them and knew exactly what had happened.

Calum walked forward. He was holding a length of metal pipe in his hand. "What happened, Luka? Your buddy not looking out for you any more?" He had to shout. The rain was getting harder, pelting down, the rumble of thunder getting closer. He had two cronies with him, rifles slung on their backs. We were all getting soaked.

I shivered, blinking water out of my eyes, and squared up to him, shouting back, "What the hell are you doing?"

"We know what you've been up to," he yelled. "Dayton knows. He's told us everything."

"Told you what?" I couldn't believe what I was hearing.

"Admit it. Admit what you've been doing. It's time to choose sides, Luka." Calum was striding around, barking mad, acting like he was on a stage, commanding a performance with a ragged pipe as a prop. He banged it against a drainpipe, pointed it at me then waved it theatrically towards the outpost. "Are you with us? Or are you with them?"

13

Water was streaming down the back of my neck. Calum's cronies moved to either side, bringing their rifles up to point at me. They weren't even standing right. Even at that range, they'd never hit me holding them like that.

I couldn't help the smile that snuck out.

Calum glowered and stepped forward. "What are you laughing at? You little shit. You're done betraying us. We don't need you any more. Don't you get it?"

He stepped in, swinging the pipe two-handed, aiming for my head. I sidestepped and shoved him. He shouldered me aside and someone grabbed me from behind, almost hauling me off my feet.

The alleyway lit up with a flash of lightning that forked across the sky.

Calum came at me again and they were holding me so all I could do was curl up as the pipe hit, taking the brunt of it on my shoulder. It stung like hell. I kicked out, clawed at the hands holding me and bit the nearest arm I could reach.

A blow landed against the back of my head, almost sending me to my knees.

Calum grabbed the front of my shirt and pulled me upright, nose to nose, rain streaming down our faces.

"You're not one of us," he screamed. "You never have been. You're Earth scum and we know what you've been doing." He was spitting rain at me.

I didn't flinch and yelled back, "What the hell am I supposed to have done?"

He gestured again, wildly, towards the outpost. "Sold us out to them."

"How?" I almost laughed again.

That didn't go down well.

He flung me around, sending me staggering backwards, as a clap of thunder crashed overhead.

He yelled something I missed as I went sprawling. I rolled splashing through puddled dirt and raised my head, shaking water off my nose, as a figure stepped out from the shadows between us, topknot unmistakable.

She had her back to me, facing up to Calum, protecting me from them, protesting, shouting, "He hasn't done anything."

The two with the rifles closed in.

"Get out of here, Freddie," Calum screamed.

I scrambled to my feet and pushed past her, grabbing her hand.

"What are you going to do?" I yelled. "Shoot us?"

Another flash lit up the city. There was a massive rumble that was too close to be thunder. I could feel the ground tremble under my feet. Gunfire started to echo through the streets. Dayton was starting his assault.

"Calum," I shouted again, trying to get Freddie behind me, "what the hell do you think I've done?"

He almost lurched at us. "You betrayed us." He looked at the kids on either side of him and yelled, "Do it."

They fired.

I ducked sideways, grabbed Freddie and ran. They missed. The shots ricocheted off the wall by my head as I barged into a doorway and shouldered open the door. I bundled her through and into darkness.

They were shouting after us. I ran, dragging her alongside me, running blind through rubble and debris, shoving our way through door after door. We burst out into another alleyway, back into the rain, and ran, hand in hand. I could hear them behind us and I could see a fire escape ladder half hanging off the side of a building up ahead. If they meant to kill us, they had a clear shot. We had no other way out but to run for it.

A shot pinged off the metal frame as we reached it. Freddie squealed. I grabbed her and hoisted her up, following as soon as I was sure it would hold us both. We scrambled onto the rooftop and ran. There was no easy way off it. I grabbed Freddie's hand as we approached the edge, running full tilt, and yelled, "Jump." We landed and rolled, skidding on the wet surface of the roof below. I lost hold of her and had to scramble back, dragging her back up into a run. She was struggling, limping and whimpering, but she kept going. We made it across two rooftops before she was done. I pulled her into the cover of an overhang and pushed a finger to her lips, mouthing, "Stay here."

I crawled out and listened, not picking up anything but the howling of the storm and the echo of gunfire in amongst the driving rain.

They could have been right on top of us and we wouldn't have known until it was too late. We couldn't stay there. We were both soaked through and shivering. Freddie was holding her ankle.

"What do they think you've done?" she said as I crawled back in.

"Calum's an idiot. I haven't done anything. Can you walk?"

"Yeah." She looked up at me. "Luka, why would they think you've betrayed us?"

I could tell from the look on her face, rain streaming down her cheeks with the tears, that she was thinking that I must have done something. That something must have happened.

I must have stiffened, pulled a face or something, because her face fell back into that dismayed look. She reached and touched my knee. "Don't look at me like that," she said. "You're one of us. I don't care what they say. I know you haven't done anything."

Problem was, I couldn't have sworn for sure that I hadn't.

"I know you haven't, Luka. That's why I followed Calum. To warn you," she said, voice small, shaking. "Peanut told me about the ore plant. Is that why we're in trouble?"

"We're not in trouble," I said. "Calum's just an idiot.

You shouldn't have followed him out here. Come on, we need to move."

We went back out into the rain and across the rooftops as fast as we could. I wanted to get her to Latia's. That was the only place I could think of to go. The thunder was still rumbling. Those storms didn't usually last long but they always got worse, much worse, before they tore themselves apart. We slid down a gutter and fell out onto a flat roof that was mostly intact. I pulled Freddie up and helped her into a run. We weren't too far from Latia's district. I couldn't feel my fingers any more. Freddie was trembling. I looked around. Unless we wanted to jump down a bomb hole, the only way I could see to get down was on the far side of the roof. We had no choice but to run out into the open.

There was a yell. Shots that pinged off the venting pipes next to us.

Freddie screamed, exhausted and about ready to collapse.

I grabbed her and pulled her back. We slipped round into the shadows and waited, listening as they yelled to each other, trying to figure out where we were. I grabbed a handful of rubble and threw it, as far as I could, watching as it hit the far wall with a clatter. They were stupid enough to fall for it, running off in the opposite direction. I gestured Freddie to be quiet, as lightning flashed in brilliant white tendrils across the sky, then we climbed up and round, back onto the higher roof.

Calum was standing there, waiting. He narrowed his eyes, a sly smile on his face, shifted his weight and hefted the pipe. Shadows moved on all sides as his cronies stepped out to surround us.

"Luka hasn't done anything," Freddie yelled, a clap of thunder drowning out her words.

I let go of her hand and moved, going for Calum as fast as he was coming at me. I ducked the pipe and got in the first punch. He went down but one of his buddies swung the rifle like a club. Right in my face.

I went flying, hit the ground and rolled, sprawling.

Then it all went into slow motion.

They got Freddie by the scruff of the neck and they dragged her away from me. She was protesting, kicking at them but they were too big.

They spread out. Freddie was screaming. The others were all shouting, jeering. They were still waving the rifles in the air.

Calum was on his feet, pulling something from his belt.

There was another flash of lightning.

Whatever he had in his hand glinted. The idiot had a knife.

I got up, reaching into my own pocket.

Calum held up the blade, grinning.

I heard Freddie yell, "No," and saw her twist away. There was another crash of thunder then a gunshot, a sharp crack that cut through the storm and the darkness.

Freddie staggered.

My fingers closed around the cold, hard sphere of the

grenade. Freddie turned, looked me right in the eye with terror frozen on her face, and then she was falling. I tried to catch her but I couldn't move fast enough.

Calum slammed into me and a burning heat burst in my stomach. I felt my knees going.

I clicked the primer.

Calum pushed me away from him. I couldn't help staggering backwards. I threw the grenade. There was a flash. And then my feet went out from under me.

I fell. I can remember hitting something. Pain so bad it didn't feel real. I think I might have screamed.

And that's when I bust my knee.

I didn't black out. It would have been easier if I had but I lay there in the torrential rain, feeling every spark of agonising pain. I've had worse. Compared to some of the stuff I've been through since, with the guild, that night at the bottom of that wall was a breeze. But back then, I was thirteen and it was the first time I'd really got hurt, and boy did it hurt.

I couldn't move without feeling like I was going to drop into a dark hole. I lay there, rain streaming down my face, every muscle tense, hand pressed over my stomach where the wetness was warm and sticky. I could feel every heartbeat pounding in my chest, feel it pulsing in my abdomen.

I can remember wondering if that was what it was like to die. Wondering if that's what it had felt like eight years ago when the bombs had hit our building, and my mother and grandparents, and my uncles and all my cousins and all those other people had died. It had been raining that night too. Did bad things always happen in the rain and the dark? I could see every detail of it, relive every minute I was trapped there in the rubble as everyone faded and died around me. I could hear every voice and cry, every whisper that got quieter and quieter until there was nothing but my heartbeat in the darkness.

Lying there that night at the bottom of the wall, I did anything to stop thinking about it. I started counting, worked out volumes of water, volumes of blood, fluid dynamics and how much I reckoned I was losing by the minute.

I lay there forever, calculating distances and fuel consumption, trying to work out if I knew enough about flying a ship yet to steal one and get everyone away from there. I was expecting Calum to turn up and finish the job. I had no idea what he thought I'd done, why Dayton would think I'd done anything to betray them. I'd just given them exactly what he'd sent me in there after. I tried to backtrack over every second of it all, figure out if I'd screwed up, if I'd done something so terrible they could see it that way, and every time I came back to nothing.

I started to fade out, grey closing in but then I heard shouting. I tensed, adrenaline pulsing. If Calum turned up and held a gun to my head, there was absolutely nothing I could do.

14

The shouting was joined by the noise of engines and weapons, far away, and then a voice really close up, yelling in my ear. Not Calum. I blinked.

Someone took hold of my wrist and someone pressed down hard on my stomach. There was a sting and the pain went sky high so bad it took my breath away, then just as suddenly, I couldn't feel anything any more. I felt my knee well enough when they tried to move me and I think I screamed again.

"Give the kid something to knock him out, for Christ's sake," someone shouted.

I felt another sharper sting on my neck and I drifted off on a cloud.

I woke up in the medical bay again. When I was in there with concussion, everyone had seemed really pissed at me. That second time, when I was really hurt, they were different, way more protective somehow, as if there were degrees of being hurt and if it was bad enough, it didn't matter what you'd done to end up there. That seems to be a trick I've got away with a lot since then.

There were more people around that time too. They were hustling with wounded and I caught snatches of conversations, talk of bombs and casualties, medical supplies being low and where the hell were the reinforcements.

It was hard not to feel guilty.

I was polite whenever any of the medics checked on me and I lay there listening, trying to figure out what I could move. There was a line in my arm again. My left knee was firmly immobilised in a brace. My stomach was sore but everything else seemed fine.

I slept a lot and one time when I was only half awake, I thought I could hear Charlie, but he wasn't there when I opened my eyes.

Then for the first time since I'd got there, I woke and felt fully awake, different, more aware, the IV line gone.

There were quiet voices beyond the curtain. They were talking about me and that time it was Charlie. He was arguing, soft tones like they were trying to keep quiet but he was pissed about something.

"No," a woman said, quiet but firm.

"He's one of ours," I heard Charlie say. "Just look at him."

"We're at our limit here," she said. "The kid is good to go. We can't keep him just because, yes, I agree, in all likelihood, he is probably the bastard sprog of some grunt who could have been here for one tour thirteen or fourteen years ago. The kid has family here. We're releasing him today."

Charlie sounded desperate. "We're still fighting out there."

"I know," she said. "That's why we're at our limit. I'm letting him go."

There were footsteps, walking away, then he pulled back the curtain and stood there. He looked like he'd been working back to back shifts. He had that tang of dust and dirt and explosives hanging around him.

I sat up and said, "Hey."

He forced a smile.

"I'm fine," I said. "I need to go. Is it okay if I go?"

He nodded.

There was a pile of clothes on the end of the bed. Desert colours, stuff the soldiers wore off-duty. I guessed that my clothes had been trashed. I shrugged into a tee shirt that was way too big.

"It's the smallest we could find," Charlie said. "Here let me help."

He got me up and dressed. The shorts were big but not stupidly so. The pack of cards was lying there on the bed. It was bulky somehow, like it had been soaked and then dried out. He must have rescued it for me. It meant a lot and I didn't know how to say it. I stuffed it into a pocket.

My sneakers were there and he helped me into them and grabbed some crutches.

"You know how to use these?" he asked.

"I'll manage."

"No climbing." He said it with a smile in his eyes.

I almost smiled back. "I'll be fine."

He looked serious all of a sudden. "Will you be fine?"

I looked at him, not sure what he was asking.

"You need to keep the brace on for at least three weeks," he said. "The knee was dislocated. You haven't broken anything but there's ligament damage. Don't walk on it. The stab wound…" He paused, looking at me as if he wanted to ask what the hell had happened. He didn't. "That should heal up okay. Keep it clean." He took a bag off the table in there. "There's trauma patches in here in case it opens up again and there are antibiotics and painkillers. Go easy on them. There's enough in there to last you a while. You run out, you don't need to steal any more. Just come tell me. Okay?"

I nodded.

"Will you be okay?"

I took the bag and nodded.

"Come on then." He turned away.

I didn't move.

He realised I wasn't following and turned back, looked at the way I was standing and said, "What?"

I bit my lip. I didn't want to ask but I couldn't not. "There were other kids up on the roof with me…"

He stared at me then said quietly, "There was a girl…" He shook his head slightly.

I sucked it up and packaged it away, the way I'd learned to eight years before. Life sucks. Losing people sucks. If you were afraid of it, it killed what time you had with the people you did have. I had no idea what Calum and the rest of them thought I'd been doing. I hadn't betrayed them. Yet there I was, standing in the Imperial base, wearing an Imperial uniform. I might as well have.

Charlie gave me a lift out to a checkpoint, as far downtown as he could go. They had defences set up, coils of wire and barricades blocking the road. He helped me out and waited while I juggled the crutches.

It was hot, the sun right overhead so it was around midday.

I squinted up at him. "Thank you," I said. Then for some reason, I added, "If he hasn't already, Dayton's going to hit the outposts."

Charlie was standing by the jeep, leaning one elbow on the open door. "We know."

"They think they can take back the mines."

He frowned. "We didn't know that."

It felt like I was never going to see him again.

I shifted my weight, the knee starting to complain. "If you haven't already, you need to change your codes."

I turned to go before he could say anything else. I could feel him staring at my back as I made my way down the street. It was quiet but an ominous quiet, too quiet. Midday, this part of town? There should have been people around, going to the market or home from school, but not a soul.

I headed into the shade. I didn't even know what day it was or how long I'd been in the garrison.

It must have taken me over an hour to get to Latia's place. My back was drenched with sweat and my stomach felt like it had a knot stitched into it.

I leaned heavier and heavier on the crutches, hands sore, counting each step and thinking of a soft bed and a cold drink. Lemonade. Latia would never let me have beer.

I knew something was wrong as soon as I saw the door was open.

My great-grandmother never left the door open. If I could have thrown away the crutches and run, I would have sprinted. I could hardly breathe by the time I pushed the door open, yelling for her, desperately wanting her to call me back and ask why such fretting, everything was fine.

Except it wasn't. I stopped in the doorway and stared. Chairs were overturned, a vase smashed on the floor. She'd never leave it in such a mess. I had a lump in my throat as I hobbled into the living room, pushing past the curtain, half expecting to find her on the floor.

There was no sign of her. I searched the whole house, top to bottom, almost falling on the stairs, shouting her name the whole time. I looked in the back yard and checked the alley, a heavy sick feeling settling over the ache in my stomach.

I limped back inside, awkward with the crutches, and was heading into the living room, no idea what I was going to do, before I realised there was someone else in the house. Heavy footsteps.

I turned as someone grabbed me from behind and flung me round, off my feet. The bag went flying, pill bottles skittering across the floor. I yelled as my knee twisted, off balance, trying to swing the crutch at them, anything to get free. I hit something. The grip loosened and I thought I was going to fall but there was a vicious curse and a fist punched into my stomach. I folded, vision closing in to a grey tunnel.

My right knee hit the floor. They had me by the scruff of my neck but there was no way they were taking me. I twisted free, the shirt tearing. I abandoned the crutches and scrambled away. I knew Latia's house back to front with my eyes closed. I slid under a table, made a break for the side door, crawling, and slipped through before they could catch me. I kicked the door shut with my right foot, pain firing through my stomach and my left leg screaming at me. It locked. I could hear them shouting to each other.

I thought I was going to be sick.

I dragged myself up, elbowed open the window and fell more than climbed through it.

There was a gate at the far end of the alley. I grabbed one of Latia's plant pots and threw it. It shattered, nudged the gate just enough for it to swing open, and I crawled behind the broken fridge unit she had out there.

I heard them bang open the back door, yell and thunder down the alley.

I leaned my head back against the hot bricks of the wall. The gate swung shut. And it was quiet.

I waited until it was dark before I made a move. I managed to limp back inside and grab my crutches. I started to scrabble about for the drugs and stuff that had spilled across the floor, but I heard footsteps outside and split, abandoning all but a handful I shoved into my pocket.

I headed to the last place we'd been holed up, hanging out in the shadows each time I heard a voice or the echo of a footstep or engine. Each time I stopped, it got harder and harder to move again. But I made it, climbed the stairs one agonising step at a time, and collapsed in a heap in a corner, one off the top floor, in our old bunkroom where there was still a mattress.

The pain in my knee was unbearable, the grubby tee shirt specked with fresh blood. I think I almost sat there and cried but I squeezed my eyes shut instead and pretty much passed out.

15

I came round slowly, vaguely aware of my knee then my stomach, both throbbing in time with my heartbeat. It wasn't terrible pain, worse than uncomfortable, but not as bad as agonising.

Until I tried to move.

And that's when I realised there was someone there with me. I hadn't heard her come in. It was too dark to see but I knew it was her. She was snuggled into me, one leg tangled into mine, one arm thrown over my chest, hugging a blanket she must have pulled over us. I was too hot and my stomach was cramping but I tried not to move so I wouldn't wake her.

She smelled clean. I wasn't. I was dusty, sweaty, sore and aching.

I held out as long as I could then I had to shift my butt to ease the pins and needles that were sparking in my leg. She stirred and murmured something. I swear I tried to not wake her but the more I thought about it, the more uncomfortable I was and the more my leg felt like it was ablaze.

I moved, she jerked awake and we both cried out as she tried to fend me off and I tried to stifle a scream as my knee took her full weight.

She hugged me then and held onto me as if she'd never let go.

"We thought you were really dead this time," she whispered into my ear.

"They killed Freddie." It was an effort to form the words coherently.

"I know."

I pulled away.

It was too dark to see her properly but I could tell she was trying not to cry.

"They took Latia," I said, heart in my stomach, hardly wanting to ask if Maisie knew anything about her.

"I know," she said. "Luka, I'm sure she's fine. Dayton's holding her because he wants you. He's told everyone to find you. He's saying…" She touched my cheek.

I batted her hand away. "He's saying what?" I almost knew what she was going to say.

"I don't believe any of it. Calum's just been waiting for something like this."

We sat there quietly then I had to lie back down because my stomach was cramping again. It didn't feel good, I didn't feel good, but I didn't want to switch on a flashlight to check it.

I stretched out. Dayton wouldn't dare hurt Latia. And my great-grandmother could give as good as she got. Good luck to them if they thought they'd be able to hold her. She'd be giving them hell.

"How did you get away?" I said.

"How do you think?" Maisie grinned at me. "They let

me go," she admitted. "They sent me off on an errand. I'm sure they thought I'd lead them straight to you."

There was no chance of that.

She placed her hand on my leg. "Is it broken?"

"Dislocated," I said. "Maisie, what's Dayton saying?"

She sucked in a breath. "Luka, I know it's not true."

"What's he saying?"

She leaned down and kissed me. First time it was anything more than a peck on the cheek. And I was half delirious and could hardly move. I tried to respond but I think I ended up whimpering.

I could feel her lips against mine, curving into a smile. She pulled away and put her hand to my forehead. "You're burning up."

"I'm fine," I muttered. "Don't stop."

She jostled me with a laugh and snuggled in again. "What are we going to do? You can't go anywhere near the tunnels. Dayton's ordered his guys to shoot you on sight."

Shoot me? I would have felt special or something if I hadn't been feeling so rubbish.

My eyes were heavy, closing even though I was fighting it. "You shouldn't be here."

"I'm not going to leave you alone. They think I'm out scavenging codes. No one can do it like you used to. I don't understand why they've turned against you."

I didn't understand it either.

She reached her arm around me and as her hand brushed my stomach, it hurt so much I cried out again.

She lifted my shirt, touched gently at the dressing and cursed. "You need medicine."

I managed to mumble, "Charlie gave me some but I left it at Latia's."

"Don't go back there, whatever you do. They've got people watching it. I'll get you something." She placed her hand so gently on my cheek I almost thought I was imagining it. "Don't go anywhere."

I almost laughed at the thought of even moving but she kissed me again.

And when I opened my eyes, she was gone. Sunlight was creeping round the corner of the window. I didn't know how long it had been, a couple of hours or a couple of days. It felt like my whole body was on fire.

One of the other kids was there. She squeezed my hand, said something that sounded like, "We've got you, don't worry," and I sank back under again.

The next time I came round, it was darker. Dusk. I felt like me again. Sore, tired, soaked in sweat like I'd been running for miles, but normal. The weird thing about being so off your head is that you don't have any idea how bad it is. And when you get back, you can't remember how bad it really was.

I leaned up on one elbow. There was a figure standing there in the shadows by the open window, tall, rifle held casually balanced in his hand, and I froze for a second before I recognised him. It was freaky seeing an adult in our domain. Even if it was in a place we'd abandoned.

Charlie turned and looked down at me, shaking his head like he was more unimpressed with me than he'd ever been.

He came over and crouched by my side, resting the rifle across his knee.

"You gotta stop breaking into the garrison," he said.

"I'm fine, thank you." I couldn't help the grin.

"I know you are." He was trying not to smile. "We just spent two days pumping you full of antibiotics and fluids. Thank Maisie. If that girl hadn't found you…"

"I know."

"Seriously, kid, stay away from the garrison."

I stretched out my leg. I needed to get up and move about but going back to sleep was also tempting. "How did you know?"

"We know everything."

I didn't believe that but I started backtracking over every single time I'd been in there, trying to figure out if I'd missed something, left a trace somewhere.

"Don't worry," he said. "We know. They don't."

I didn't have a clue what that meant.

"How do you do it?" he asked casually as if he was asking how I tied my shoes.

"Do what?"

He took a code book out of his pocket and tossed it open onto my lap.

I stared at it then looked him in the eye. "I didn't always give them everything."

"We know. I want to know how you do it."

There was something about Charlie. There always had been. And it hadn't just been that thunderstorm and the poker game. I'd met Charlie when I was only five. He was the one who had pulled me from the rubble that had once been my home.

I trusted him and I didn't even think about why I shouldn't.

I closed the book, hardly giving it a second's glance, and handed it back to him, starting to reel off the code from the page it had opened at.

It took him a second to open it again, frowning until he caught up with me and started reading along. Then he shook his head with a smile.

He turned back a few pages. "What about seven thirty four?" he said.

I started but he interrupted.

"Three twenty two."

I started again.

"Alright, alright, I get it. Have you still got the cards?"

I nodded, desperately hoping he wouldn't ask for them back.

"You always let me win, didn't you?" he said.

I nodded again.

He laughed. "Jesus. Don't ask me to play poker with you again." He looked serious then. "Stay away from Dayton. You understand?" He stood. "Stay put. I'm gonna get you out of here."

I really wanted to believe him so I didn't argue.

He went to the window.

I threw off the blanket as he turned away, struggling to my feet and grabbing the crutches to follow him.

The city was quiet.

"We're holding," he said, "but they're regrouping."

He said it like I was one of his now. And the way he said 'holding' was desperate. Earth didn't station many troops on Kheris at any time. They'd been wiped out, severely depleted, and the UM forces were still buzzing all around the crashed ship, right on our doorstep. He'd come to help me even though they must have been run off their feet.

Charlie watched for a second then turned to me. "We've got reinforcements coming in," he said. "They'll be here soon. I need to know where you are. We might have to move out fast. You stay here. You understand?"

And he turned to go.

Maisie was there in the doorway. She let him pass then stared at me. I was guessing she'd heard what he'd said earlier.

"I'm not going anywhere without you," I said.

She didn't say anything but I could tell from the haunted look in her eye that she didn't believe me.

I didn't know what else to say. We stared at each other for a minute then she gave me that look and climbed out onto the window ledge. I managed to get out there to sit next to her and we sat there, watching UM blitz the crash site. Peanut turned up and sat with us, his eyes glued to his field glasses, giving us a running commentary.

They didn't come anywhere near the city. The alarms had all stopped, no gunfire within the walls. It was as if everyone was watching what was going on out there.

I was sitting with my leg stretched out, leaning against the wall, feeling the heat from the day on my back, the cool breeze of the night on my face. No one had said it yet but they needed to go. They were all risking themselves being there with me.

"You should be getting back," I said to Maisie finally. I wanted to ask her to stay but that wasn't fair. I should have done. Maybe if I had, everything would have worked out differently.

"Promise me you'll be careful." She didn't look at me as she said it. "Dayton has people out looking for you."

"I'll be fine. See if you can talk to Latia, will you?"

"I will." She looked at me then, with that set to her jaw, then she climbed back inside and disappeared. I thought she might have kissed me again if Peanut hadn't been there. But he was. So she didn't.

We sat there for a while longer. I was thinking I needed to move, find somewhere new to hole up but I wasn't sure I could make it down the stairs. I had no idea how I'd even made it up there.

"If you want her," Peanut said suddenly without lowering the glasses, "you're going to have to work harder than that."

"What?"

He turned sharply to look at me, laughed, then turned back to his scrutiny of the conflict going on out there.

"Maisie," he said. "You want her, it's going to take more effort than lying there looking all hurt and vulnerable."

"I don't know what you mean," I said. I might have blushed. I'm still not sure I totally understand what it was Peanut told me that night.

"You want that girl, Luka," he said, "you have to earn her. Sure, you can pull off all the daring stunts you want. Be the bad boy, the hero. Smile at them all cute-like all you want and they'll fall for you. But you want Maisie? You really want a girl that special? Then think about what she needs. And don't compromise. Don't even think beyond what she needs, whatever she might tell you. Either that or get her chocolate. And I don't mean that crap you steal off your Earth buddies. You want Maisie? I'll get you some real chocolate."

I stared at him.

"It's tough getting the older woman," he said with a laugh. "Trust me. Now take a look at this shit that's going on out there and tell me what you make of it."

I took the field glasses and adjusted the field of vision, scanning round until I saw the ship. The UM ground troops were surrounding it but holding off. I almost held my breath, half expecting what had happened to the Earth troops to happen again. It made me feel cold just thinking about it.

"They can't get in," Peanut said. "They dump all that ordinance on it and they still can't get in."

I sat back. "Dayton's probably out there, trying to make some kind of deal with them."

Peanut took back the glasses and yawned. "Dayton doesn't give a shit about this place," he said. "I thought you knew that."

I opened my mouth to reply but Peanut swore softly and swung the glasses down towards the street. We had incoming.

16

I followed the direction he was looking and could just about make out four or five figures, a couple of adults with three kids, all with rifles.

"That's Calum," Peanut said. He jumped down off the window ledge. "Come on. Can you make it across the rooftops?"

It's incredible what adrenaline can do for you. We clattered up the stairs, hearing shouts below us, Calum yelling my name in amongst a string of obscenities. There were other voices. More shouting.

"Who else is here?" I managed to say, not realising how out of breath I was until I tried to talk.

"Don't worry about them," Peanut said over his shoulder. "Dayton just wants you."

We made it to the landing, one level off the roof, footsteps thundering up behind us, and he grabbed my shoulder and pulled me aside, backing through a doorway and pushing me into a corner, holding his finger to his lips, eyes piercing into mine.

I got the message and held still, trying to breathe, trying to keep it quiet, and struggling not to slump down in a heap.

He gestured, beckoning, and I handed over one of the

crutches, guessing what he was getting at, and I stood there, twirling the other into a two-handed grip as if it was a staff, as if I had any chance of hitting anyone with it balancing on one leg.

We waited there, hiding.

We could hear Calum still swearing as he ran up and past us, going on up to the roof, the others following him.

My heart was thumping so hard it felt like they'd be able to hear it a mile away.

Peanut glanced at me, then the door, then the floor. I could almost hear his brain trying to work out if they'd all gone past. I shook my head. There was still one to go.

We couldn't hear him.

We watched as the door pushed open, slowly, a gun barrel appearing, the beam from the flashlight taped to it scanning round the room.

Peanut was bracing himself for a fight. I was just trying not to fall over. If this guy took two steps into the room and turned around, he'd see us.

He didn't. He backed out and moved off up the stairs, almost without a sound, leaving us in total darkness again.

I carefully lowered the crutch to the ground and leaned on it, taking the pressure off my knee. Peanut was shaking his head, cursing silently under his breath. He handed me the other, his finger on his lips again, and headed across the room.

I limped after him to the balcony and stared out at the gaping abyss of darkness between the buildings as if it had stretched by half a mile overnight.

It was an easy jump. Should have been a cinch. And I knew I couldn't make it. Not as I was.

I looked at Peanut and he knew it.

"Climb down?" he mouthed.

I peered over the edge. I'd done it a hundred times before. It was the first time I can ever remember being wary of doing something and I hated it. I hated that feeling of incapacitating anxiety that clutched at the pit of my stomach. I drew on every reason I'd ever had to never be afraid of anything ever again and shook it off. Sucked it up and fed off it instead.

I shook my head and mouthed back, "Up."

He looked at me like I was insane as I ditched the crutches and hoisted myself up onto the railings. I could only take my weight on one leg and the weakness in my stomach muscles was pulling me sideways but my arms were fine and there was nothing wrong with my right leg. I climbed up to the next ledge and sat waiting for him. There was an overhang so even if they looked down from the roof, they wouldn't see us.

We could hear them up there. We sat tight and waited while they searched, watching the thin arcs of light dance over the neighbouring buildings as they cast their searchlights around trying to spot us. They didn't waste much time before they started to yell to each other to get back down.

We waited until it was all quiet then climbed up. My arms were screaming at me by the time we crawled out onto the roof. Peanut helped me up, we turned and froze.

The figure standing there had his rifle up and pointing at us. He'd turned the flashlight off so it was just us and him, all standing there in the shadows. There was something familiar about him.

We must have stood there like that for an age then he lowered the gun and took a step forward.

"If you really are working for them, Luka," he said, voice low, "then go, get inside their walls and stay there, because next time, I might not be able to let you go."

I should have kept my mouth shut but you know what I'm like. I blurted out, "Benjie, why the hell do you even think that?" I was standing there, still wearing the clothes Charlie had given me in the garrison, wearing their colours, their insignia on the sleeve. It was stupid to even try to protest but that's hindsight for you. Idiots like Calum hated me because I was good at stuff. I think I was hoping that Benjie was different.

He brought the rifle up again. "It doesn't matter what I think."

I thought he was going to pull the trigger but he dropped the stance and turned. Walked away without another word.

I felt Peanut shiver.

"Are the kids still with Calum?" I said quietly.

"Shit," he whispered. "Yes, they are. I took the bolt off that damn cupboard door."

I didn't know what to say.

Peanut shook his head. "We need to get the kids away from them."

I felt sick beyond the tiredness and injuries. "Peanut," I said. "I'm not… I've never…"

He cut me off. "Don't." He looked me in the eye for a long moment as if he was going to say something profound. He didn't. "Stay here," he said instead. "Right here," and banged his hand against the vent making me jump. "I'll check they've gone."

I guessed it wasn't going well when he didn't reappear. I couldn't hear anything from the building below. Gunfire and shouts were echoing through the city, sounds of combat drifting in from the desert. I was starting to chill down. My clothes were sticking to me. I should have changed, showered, eaten, tried to rescue Latia, kissed Maisie again… It's stupid what runs through your head when you're hurting and trapped on top of a building by people you used to think were on your side.

I slunk further and further back into the dark as I waited. If they ran back up to the roof, there was nowhere to go. Whenever I broke into the garrison, I always had a get out planned, wherever I was. There on the roof? Nada.

I think I jerked awake when I heard the noise at the edge. I wasn't asleep on my feet but I wasn't far from it. I had to work to slow my breathing, keep quiet, squeeze deeper into the scant cover I had.

I knew who it was as soon as I saw her climb up and roll into a crouch, and I started to shiver.

She looked around, looked right towards me without seeing me and started to turn away.

"Wait, Maisie, wait," I hissed and limped out, wary still and looking around but if I couldn't trust Maisie, I really was screwed.

She ran to me and grabbed me in a hug, dragged me back into cover and pressed a finger to my lips with a shush. "You can't stay here," she whispered. "They're going to search the whole block. Dayton has this whole area back under his control. We need to go across the rooftops." She stared at me, not wanting to ask if I could make it.

"I'm good," I whispered back, shivering uncontrollably and giving her a grin to show I meant it. "Where's Peanut?"

She glared at me with sparks in her eyes. "I don't know. Dayton's guys are everywhere. They're going for the mines. Everyone's saying UM turning up gives us everything we need. They're going for it, Luka. This is it. They're going to take back the colony."

She shushed me again when I tried to argue and said again that we had to go. I let her lead me across the roof, feeling her fingernails digging into my skin as she gripped my arm.

I had to bite my lip to divert the pain from my knee, pins of red heat stabbing into it with each faltering step. She caught me when I stumbled and took me right to the edge. "Can you climb down?" she whispered.

I shook my head. "Need to jump from here." I wanted to unstrap the brace from my knee, but I knew it wouldn't hold without it.

"What's wrong?"

"I can't move with this on."

I bent to undo the catch.

She caught hold of my hand to stop me. "No. You can."

They could have appeared at any minute but it felt like we had all the time in the world and, standing there with her on that rooftop, it felt like the whole world was ours and we were the only people in it. She stood there, holding my arm and looking right into my soul. I took hold of her and held her tight, holding the back of her neck, kissing her and not caring if she was going to kiss me back or not. She did. There was no hesitation.

We stayed like that, together for what felt like forever then I pulled away and whispered in her ear, "You go first. I might need you to catch me."

She laughed, staring me in the eye before turning and running for the edge.

I watched her land and roll to her feet on the other side. I sucked in a breath, got my balance and ran.

Have you ever experienced pain so bad that all you can do is parcel it up and move away from it? Laugh at it like it's not yours so you can float above it and ignore it.

Every step was agonising. I jumped off my right leg, pushed off and knew straight away it wasn't enough. It was a jump I'd made loads of times, no big deal, and I blew it.

I fell.

It was astonishingly quiet. I twisted and reached out, bumping my hand against anything it could reach. I hit a ledge and tumbled, trying to grab something, scraping my hand across a railing before I managed to hold on. My arm locked, I hit the wall and I bounced back, hanging there, full weight on one tenuous grip, three straining fingers between me and a fifty foot fall to the ground.

I had to swing to get my other hand up there before I could climb and scramble my way up onto the balcony, hauling myself up and crawling past broken plant pots to sprawl on my back, laughing or crying, it could have been either.

Maisie dropped down beside me and thumped me in the arm. "You shit," she hissed. "You did that on purpose."

I curled up, fending her off with a grumble. "I think I broke my arm."

She looked horrified, concerned and outraged in fast succession as I couldn't help laughing. She thumped me again and pulled me up.

"Hey," I muttered as she took off, dragging me after her, "I can't walk that fast."

"Suck it up, Luka," she muttered back at me. "There's three more jumps you're gonna have to make."

17

We made it past Dayton's guys before she let me stop. I was leaning heavier and heavier on her, couldn't bear to put even the tiniest amount of weight on my knee. We staggered into one of the abandoned stores and she let me sink down in a corner.

"We can't stay here," she said, pulling a pack off her back and rummaging. I thought she might have food but she just got out a bottle of water and a popper sheet of pills. She handed them over. "Take some of these."

I didn't ask what they were. Anything was welcome. I downed a couple and sat back. "There's a place on Seventh I could go. You need to get back."

She looked at me like I was insane. "I'm not going back and you can't stay anywhere. I'm taking you to Charlie. He said he'd get you out of here. He said that, didn't he?"

I kept quiet. He had said that but they were on high alert. They had the resistance kicking off and UM on their doorstep. The security status must have gone through the roof. Charlie wouldn't have time to worry about a stray kid who'd been stupid enough to get himself kicked out of his little gang, who was stupid enough not to stay put when told to.

Anyway, I wouldn't go anywhere without Latia.

I didn't say anything but Maisie was smart enough to figure out what I was thinking.

I scuffed my right foot through the dust, left leg stretched out, the knee throbbing and swollen. The rest of me was just tired. I didn't know how I was going to move again.

"We need to get the kids away from Calum," I said instead.

"I know. If not Charlie, then where?"

"Seventh. I used to go to this place there when I was bunking out of that shit school. No one uses it."

She didn't look happy but she leaned in, gave me a kiss on the cheek and dragged me to my feet.

"We'll get out of here," she said. "All of us."

The sky was starting to brighten by the time we got there. It was an old bar that had been hit by a stray shell eight years ago. Like most of this part of the city, no one had been interested in repairing it and it had been abandoned.

She left me there. Just a hug that time. I watched her go from the doorway.

I didn't feel safe enough to sleep but I could hardly keep my eyes open. I made it up to the top floor where the roof had caved in and sat in amongst the rubble, watching the school across the street and the outpost guarding the junction at the end of the road. There was a guard on duty up there but no one else around. Dayton's crowd wouldn't come anywhere near this part of town. Not openly. Some of them lived out in the city, drank in the bars, met in the cafes and bakeries. I'd heard them talking about their lives. As if the tunnels and the resistance was just a job they went to afterhours. But they wouldn't come after me out here in force. Not in daylight.

I sat there watching as the sun rose and the city woke up and hurried about its business. Life goes on, even in a war zone. The place I was in wasn't that bad. I reckoned if Dayton did try to get to me there, I could make a break for the outpost. They might take me in. Or even the school.

I had no idea what Maisie was planning to get the kids away from Calum. Just the little ones, we'd agreed. Only the ones we knew for sure wouldn't side with him. The ones he could use against me like he had Freddie.

It was tough waiting. I should have been down there with them but she was right, I was no good to anyone if I was dead.

I started planning how I could get Latia out, working out scenarios and what ifs, then I got the cards out and practised shuffling the deck, messing about. Once it got to midday, I started to get worried and worked my way back down to ground level to stand just inside the doorway, watching. I reckoned something was up when the troops at the outpost came out and started to patrol, warning people off the streets. It wasn't often they threw out curfew orders in the middle of the day but it wasn't unheard of. The school hadn't even opened. I'd lost track of what day it was so I had no idea if it was even supposed to. It had crossed my mind that there would be food in there, but I didn't want to disappear in case I missed Maisie. I kept thinking she'd turn up any minute.

When she did, she was running. She had a bunch of the little ones with her, one of them balanced on her hip, my crutches in her other hand. A fairly stiff wind was blowing in from the desert and the kids were struggling in the heat and dust. I couldn't see any of Dayton's guys behind them, a couple of city folk scurrying up the road but no one with guns out, no one obviously chasing them. I limped out to meet her, let one of the youngsters clamber up onto my back and struggled along beside her, taking the crutches as she held them out to me.

"What's going on?"

She was herding the kids as fast as they'd go. "Dayton's attacking the mine. I'm going back for Latia. You need to get everyone inside." She handed me the one she was carrying.

With the crutches, I could hardly handle one, never mind two. They clung on, their little hands around my neck. I slowed. "Wait. Let me come with you."

"You can't," she said. "Calum's out looking for you. He'll…"

She was cut off as the ground shook with the force of a massive explosion. Another, even bigger, followed. The kids starting screaming. I looked around. A dust cloud was billowing up into the sky, way out in the desert, opposite direction to the crashed ship, but the shockwave had rippled through the ground under our feet.

Maisie glanced round at me.

"Oh shit," I said.

She looked horrified. "The processing plant?"

"It must have been."

We stood there out on the street, wide open, soldiers from the outpost starting to turn and look at us.

"We should get inside," I muttered.

We'd taken two steps then the warning siren started to wail. My stomach turned to ice. It felt like time stood still. Maisie looked at me. We'd both heard that siren before.

We started to move.

"Where do we go?" she yelled. "The school?"

I was trying to keep up, not going fast enough. The last time the gas warning had sounded, we'd been with Latia and she'd taken us all to the shelter on her block, calmly telling us it had happened before and it would happen again, and it was nothing to be afraid of, they used such dangerous chemicals to process our ores, why else did we think they'd build such lovely shelters? I'd always thought they were for the air raids. We'd huddled there in the dark, listening to her stories and eating the candy from ration packs while we waited for the all clear.

"It's closed," I shouted back between breathless gasps.

"So where? Where's the nearest shelter?"

"The outpost."

It looked way off.

I glanced behind us. The dust cloud was blowing into the city.

I yelled, "Go. Get to the outpost."

I couldn't move any faster. Maisie was trying to drag the others into a run. They were all crying. People behind us were shouting. The soldiers up ahead were shouting. And the whole time, the siren was wailing. We couldn't move fast enough. The last time, when we'd come up out of the airtight shelter, the streets had been littered with dead bugs and dead birds. The wind was blowing it right at us and we couldn't move fast enough. I knew it, from the distance and the wind speed. I almost pulled up and stopped trying to run but one of the kids had hold of my arm and was pulling me along.

I looked behind us again. At the far end of the street, people who'd been taken by surprise, caught in the open, were starting to drop, bodies falling to the road. Maisie was screaming at me. More of the soldiers were appearing, shouting, a couple of them breaking away and running towards us.

My eyes were watering, each breath getting harder.

I didn't recognise Charlie until he was right there beside me, taking the little ones I was carrying and shouting to one of the others to get that kid inside. I didn't know what he talking about. I tried to see where Maisie was but someone grabbed me and lifted me off my feet. I started yelling but they just ran, threw me over their shoulder and ran. My head was spinning, grey closing in, each pounding footstep driving hammers into my skull.

It got dark, cool. I felt myself falling, dumped on the ground. I rolled and tried to get to my feet. I thought I was going to throw up. Someone reached a hand to my shoulder but I shrugged them off. There was shouting ahead of me. I blinked through the tears, trying to see, stumbling forward. People were at the door, shouting. I could hear Maisie screaming. There was an automated voice counting down, warning us to stand clear.

Charlie was still out there.

I could see him running, carrying two of the kids, pulling another behind him. He was shouting.

Maisie was in the doorway, fighting to get free from the soldier who was holding her there, Spacey with them, just standing screaming.

I pushed my way through. Everyone was shouting, willing them to get in.

In a heartbeat, the countdown stopped. Someone yanked me backwards.

And the door slammed shut.

18

My heart was in my throat. One of the other soldiers began hammering at the override, swearing at the damned AI to open up.

I struggled free and threw myself at the door. Charlie and the others were four steps away. I could see them through the window.

"Get it open," I yelled. I spun round. "They're right here. Get it open."

The guy was thumping at the override.

Three steps.

"Toxicity levels high," the AI was saying over the comm unit. "Facility secure."

We were all screaming at it to open the door.

Two steps.

The dust cloud was right behind them. It swirled.

I yelled again. The soldier next to me was swearing, ripping the panel off the wall to get to the controls.

Charlie stumbled to one knee, trying to shelter the kids, drawing them close and falling as the dust enveloped them. It crashed against the door, turning the window orange.

I stood, staring, numb.

It was deathly quiet in there.

The AI said again in its clipped voice, "Toxicity levels high. Facility secure."

I couldn't move.

I've never trusted an AI since.

Someone took me by the shoulder and led me away. They gave us oxygen. Maisie sat opposite me. She had Spacey on her knee, hugging her tight. I stared at them over the top of the mask, still struggling to breathe, eyes still watering.

No one talked to us. Someone gave us meds, to counter the effects of any gas we might have been exposed to, I overheard someone say.

I felt sick. People were moving all around us. It blurred into slow motion. My vision closed in and my reality flashed back to that dark night and the pouring rain. The screams, the explosions. The cold and paralysing fear. I started to shiver and I couldn't stop.

I was so lost, it felt like I would never find my way back but a gentle insistent whisper filtered through somehow and enticed me back to the outpost. Maisie had her arm around me. Someone had thrown a blanket over our shoulders. I leaned in to her and cried.

The outpost was kept under lockdown for about sixteen hours. We weren't the only civilians in there. There was a woman I recognised as one of the schoolteachers from across the road and two people I hadn't seen before. We sat in a corner and they stared at us. Spacey kept asking where the others were like she'd forgotten what had happened already. She was four or five and I couldn't look at her without thinking that was how small I'd been back then.

Even when the all clear was given, they didn't let us go. I could hear the schoolteacher talking to the soldiers about us. Maisie and Spacey were asleep, curled up on a bench.

I stared into nothing.

After a while, one of the soldiers walked up. He was wearing battle armour, sergeant's stripes, and for a second I thought it was Charlie and it was as if nothing had happened. But he took his helmet off and he had dark hair. Not Charlie. Charlie was dead.

I knew I wasn't looking terribly welcoming but I couldn't shift up a gear. It was like I'd zoned out and I didn't want to go back.

He looked at me, awkward, and crouched beside us.

"Hey," he said, like Charlie always had.

I didn't say anything.

He put a ration pack down on the bench. He looked uncomfortable, like he wasn't used to talking to kids.

I said, "Thank you," to be polite.

"You're the kid that does the numbers?"

I shrugged.

"I…" He rooted about in his pocket and I thought he was going to pull out a chocolate bar but he just pulled out his hand, clenched, and opened it, palm up, offering it to me.

It was a chain with tags.

I almost cried again but he was staring me in the eye so I sucked it up and stared back.

"Charlie didn't have any family," he said, controlled as if he was sucking it up too. "We're sure he would've wanted you to have these."

I took the tags and wrapped the chain around my hand.

"There's these as well," he said, digging out some other stuff.

It was the black band Charlie had always worn around his wrist and a pocket knife.

I took them.

The guy glanced down at Maisie and Spacey then looked back at me. "We know Charlie was trying to get you out of here. We're seeing what we can do. Okay, bud?"

I was biting my lip so bad I could taste blood. I nodded solemnly, the tags cold in my hand.

"Don't leave here. You understand?"

I nodded again.

He stood and backed off, looking at us as if he was going to say something and deciding against it.

The schoolteacher was still looking at us as he walked away.

I sat there, clutching Charlie's stuff, my heart thumping. I had his deck of cards in my pocket. It felt like I had custody of his life and I didn't know if I was big enough to do him justice.

I put everything in my pocket and stood. Maisie would kill me but I couldn't just sit there any more. Not without

Latia. And it somehow felt like if Maisie was there and she had Spacey to look after, she wouldn't be able to run out after me and she'd be safe. I just needed to go get Latia. And Peanut. And Benjie. And anyone else I could find.

The schoolteacher stood and tried to intercept me. I mumbled something about needing the bathroom and she let me go, giving me that look I'd seen before, somewhere between wanting to look after me and worrying I was going to steal something from her.

I didn't take anything from her but I did sideswipe a couple of data boards that were lying there, without anyone seeing.

There was no one else in the restroom. I locked the door and ran the tap for a bit in case anyone was listening. There was a small window in there that someone had pushed open already. I could hardly put any weight on my knee but I refastened the brace tighter, hoisted myself up and climbed out.

The air was still, a tang of bitterness to it that caught at the back of my throat. I climbed up to the roof and sat there for a minute, working out my bearings and figuring out the watch positions.

I didn't want to go round to the front. I was dreading seeing Charlie and the little ones lying there on the ground outside but they were gone and the street looked like nothing had happened.

The sun was setting. I found a place to sit and wait,

beyond any prying eyes and nowhere near any of the AI sensors. There was a constant echo of gunfire dancing around the city blocks. I stared at the tags and read the inscription, 'ANDERTON C.', with a long number and blood group etched below it. I took the knife out of my pocket and carefully scratched an 'L' before the 'C' then hooked the chain over my neck.

I sat back and watched the shadows lengthen, the sky darken, checking out the stuff on the boards. I couldn't see from there but I could still hear the UM bombardment of the crashed ship, as relentless as it had been. Gas doesn't affect combat soldiers in full powered armour. They'd know nothing of the dramas going on in our little colony. They probably didn't give a hoot about the KRM and the Empire's claim on the place. They just wanted whatever it was that had crashed out there. If it did belong to Aries, they'd probably show up soon and join the fight for it. I half hoped they would. Aries was supposed to have kick-ass gunships.

I waited until it was dark then I slid down, crept into the street, retrieved the crutches that were still lying where I'd dropped them, and I slipped away into the back alleys.

I had no idea where Dayton was holding Latia and I can't even remember what I was thinking. That I could bargain maybe? That if I gave myself up, they'd let her go. Or that I could go down there and confront them, find out why the hell they thought I'd betrayed them. I do know that I considered going to the garrison and telling them everything. If I was being accused of being a traitor, I might as well be. Screw them.

Except they had Latia and I'd never let her down.

I needed to get changed and I had clothes at Latia's place so I made my way there, avoiding Dayton's guys. They were openly out in the street, guns out, scarves drawn up over their faces, blazing braziers at every street corner. They were laughing, joking around, as if they had such a high hand that the Earth forces weren't even a threat any more.

It wasn't hard to slip past them, weird to feel like I was entering enemy territory when I was heading into what used to be home. I didn't know where I belonged any more. And what was worse, I didn't know where I wanted to belong.

They had people posted on watch all along Latia's street as well as up on the roof opposite the back alley.

I stayed low, snuck into a building three doors down and limped down into the cellars. I knew the rat runs down there with my eyes closed. There were some places I was too big to squeeze through any more but enough that I could still get through to make my way round and into Latia's.

It was dark and quiet inside her house. I could feel that there wasn't anyone in there, just that empty stillness you can sense when you walk into an unoccupied building. It was eerie. I felt like I was intruding, as if it had been years since I'd been there with her, not just a few days. My stomach felt cold.

I abandoned the crutches and crawled through to retrieve my box, rummaging with shaking hands through all my stuff until I found the small pot I was looking for. I had to force myself to close the box back up and put it away as carefully as I always had when all I wanted to do was abandon it as if none of it mattered any more. It was almost as if I knew I was never going back.

I dragged myself upstairs and limped into my old room. It felt alien, like I was intruding on someone else's life.

I emptied the pockets of the shorts onto the bed and stripped off, pausing for a second when I was half undressed to prod at the dressing taped to my stomach. It was still tender but nowhere near as bad as it had been. I was tempted to pull it off and have a look but there was a noise outside that spooked me into hurrying up.

I changed into my things, the darkest stuff I had, and wrapped Charlie's band around my forearm, feeling it constrict with a sting. Faint numbers started to scroll across its matt surface. There was the time, something that looked like a temperature reading and other stuff that meant nothing to me but it all looked cool. I pulled the sleeves down, put his knife into my pocket and grabbed the pot of camouflage paint.

I stood there, looking at it, heart pounding. I opened the lid, scooped out some of the black and rubbed it into my hair as if I could scrub out who I was.

I stared at my reflection in the dirty window and drew a thick horizontal line of black paint across each cheekbone.

The data boards were all I had that could make a difference with Dayton. I stuffed them into a backpack, pulled up the hood of my shirt, grabbed the crutches and left.

I kept to the back alleys and the shadows. It sounded like the entire southern side of the city belonged to the resistance, pretty much the whole way up to Main. I didn't see any Imperial patrols, no tanks, no gunships. I took care but I was almost daring Dayton's men to confront me. I stood at street corners and watched them, breathing in the smoke, the heightened emotions and bravado they were emanating. They were being so cocky, it would have been easy to think they had made a deal with UM.

I worked my way round, heading for one of the safe houses. I reckoned I needed to get into the tunnels. Get to Dayton himself to get him to free Latia. Something was screwy and I just needed to sort it out, make sure I didn't run into Calum or any of his cronies and just make it to the tunnels.

Even with the crutches and a busted knee, I made my way past their blockades easily. And the longer I got away with it, the more reckless I got. It was funny.

Until someone grabbed my shirt and dragged me backwards into a doorway.

19

My knee twisted and I almost screamed, biting it back and fighting them off, squirming free and backing away, turning to run, except they caught me again and spun me around, pulling me close and hissing into my ear, "Quit it, squirt. What the hell are you doing?"

I stopped struggling and stood there, chest heaving, trying to balance on the crutches to get the weight off my knee.

Benjie. Probably the only one who had a chance of predicting what I'd do and where I'd go.

He straightened me up and I thought he was going to shove me away but he grabbed me in a bear hug.

"We heard some of the kids got caught in the gas," he said quietly, his voice catching.

"Maisie and Space are alive. They're at the outpost. The others…" I couldn't say it.

He pushed me away gently, holding me by each arm. "What are you doing, Luka? It's not safe for you to be out here."

He had a rifle on his back, a gash across one eyebrow and a dirty bandage wrapped around his hand. He didn't look grown up and cool any more, he looked like a tired kid.

"I have a way out," I said. "I can get us away from here, all of us."

He stared at me, glanced away behind me out into the street, and pulled me further in to the doorway. "There is no way out. And if you get caught, Dayton is going to shoot you. Do you understand that?"

I pushed him away and scowled. "I don't understand why."

He frowned at me.

I shrugged the backpack off and pulled out one of the boards. "I've got the latest codes for him, stats on troops and everything. There's even some stuff about UM."

Benjie was looking at me like I was crazy.

"I want to trade," I said. "I want him to let Latia go. We're going to get away."

He shook his head slowly. "Won't work. Whatever you've got on there. Dayton wants you dead, Luka. You don't know why?"

I shrugged, frowning, half of me feeling ticked off and the other half planning another way in.

He didn't look impressed. "I talked to Peanut. He said you do know why. C'mon, be straight with me. If you've got something on Dayton, tell me."

"I don't have anything. Why does Peanut think I do?"

Benjie shook his head. "Think about it, kid. You've done nothing but help Dayton and help our cause. Why does he suddenly think you've betrayed him?" He paused then added, pointedly, "If you haven't."

"I haven't." Even as I said it, I felt cold. I've learned

a lot about the playing of games since I've been with the guild. That's what we do. It's all a game. Back then, I don't even think it's that I was naïve. I just wanted to fix everything.

But Dayton was playing a game. This whole thing was just because he thought I knew something about him. Something damning.

I almost laughed. "What the hell does Peanut think I have? Where is he?"

Benjie pulled the rifle round off his back. "I don't know. He split. I don't even know if he's alive."

My stomach knotted. "What?"

"Luka, I don't know."

I think I just gawped at him, heart thumping a steady numb rhythm.

He squeezed my shoulder, holding tight, looking at me the way he'd always used to whenever I'd screwed up and freaked out, and he'd had to talk me back to that steady, ever so fine line of being able to function.

"Listen to me." He squeezed tighter. "Luka, listen to me. Peanut wouldn't tell me what it was, but he said you knew and he said not to trust Dayton."

"Why would he say that?" My voice sounded hollow, stomach twisting.

Benjie screwed up his face like he was done being patient with me. "I don't know. He said you've been set up. Come on, Dayton was fine with you before you went into the comms centre. Did you get something from there? Have you told anyone?"

I shrugged, wanting to scream, run away, hit the wall, anything but stand there so numb.

"Did you take something? Come on, Luka, think."

"I took a load of crap. I didn't even look at it…" I stared at Benjie. My chest felt heavy. "I gave it all to Peanut."

His stance changed. He straightened and looked at me. "You really don't know what it is, do you?"

If it was possible, I felt even more cold. I trusted him. If I'd lost Benjie, I was done. If Benjie was digging to find out what I knew, if I knew Dayton's secret, then I could have just signed my own death warrant, right there. I almost backpedalled, but I bit my tongue and stared back at him.

He punched me in the arm. "Jesus, Luka, don't look at me like I'm the bad guy here. Where is it?"

"I gave it to Peanut," I said quietly, feeling bad that I could have doubted him.

"He didn't have it. He said you'd know where it was, somewhere safe. Where would that be?"

I didn't know what to say. My heart was racing. I was trying to think, trying to work out what I should and shouldn't have done, who I could and couldn't trust, what might lead to what and why. Latia had taught me how to play chess when I was six and it was like trying to figure out ten moves ahead.

If Benjie had dared tell me to trust him right then, I think I would have kicked him in the shin and made a run for it.

As it was, he leaned in close and took hold of my

shoulder again. "Luka, listen to me. I don't like what Dayton is doing. I don't like that he's using Calum and I don't like that he's holding Latia. If he's screwing us over, I want to take him down."

There was gunfire echoing from the far end of the street.

Latia had also taught me to always use my instincts. The knots in my stomach were tightening but I nodded.

I'd given the stuff from the comms centre to Peanut in Calum's dingy basement. There was no way Peanut would call that safe.

"Our old block," I said. "That's where he'd have left it if he wanted it safe. Why didn't he just tell you what it was?"

"You know what Peanut is like. And he didn't have much of a chance to. C'mon, we need to go and find this thing before Dayton does."

"Wait, Benjie, I need to get Latia. They've offered us a way out."

He grabbed the front of my shirt and pulled me close, leaning down and speaking quietly and intently. "Luka, listen to me. Dayton's got people searching everywhere for you. Didn't you hear what I said – he wants you dead. We need to find out what the hell he's hiding." He let me go then did a double take. "They've offered you a way out? They? The Empire? Bloody hell, Luka, don't even…" He cursed, shoved me to turn me around and I felt the weight of the rifle drop over my shoulders followed by an oversized combat helmet planted on my head. "Whatever you do, don't say that to anyone else. Can you walk without the crutches?"

I didn't think I could.

He swore. "Just follow my lead, okay?"

We made our way back to our old block, stopping a couple of times when he told me to stay back and keep out of the way so he could clear it with people, and a couple of other times at corners to warm ourselves at braziers and swap small talk.

I kept quiet and let Benjie do the talking. He sideswiped me a couple of times in front of Dayton's guys, let them see who was in charge, kept up the act of being the big guy resistance fighter. He didn't give them a chance to look too closely at me, saying stuff like, "These damned kids, who woulda thought they'd be so useful?"

They let us through, his mind games worked. On me more than them, I realised afterwards. It's weird what you can make people think and feel if you know what you want more confidently than they do. Benjie taught me something that night. I wish I'd got the chance to thank him properly.

Our old building was dark and quiet. I struggled up the stairs, half hoping Benjie would give me a hand but I guess he had problems of his own to deal with. He took the rifle and helmet back at least. Even without the weight of those, I was bent over double by the time we reached the top and he just looked at me and muttered, "Shit," under his breath, like that summarised everything we'd gone through just to get there.

I felt cold. It was the first time I really stood there and thought and I just felt cold. More than numb. That had been and gone. I felt cold. Like I didn't care but it was a burning cold, like I could spark and ignite at any minute given the right catalyst. It felt powerful. Ominous.

I knew Benjie was feeling it too.

We stood there, staring at each other, and laughed.

"You're insane," Benjie said.

I threw back the hood and stood there, my face covered with war paint, regarding him with defiance even though I could barely stand up straight. "I haven't betrayed anyone."

He regarded me with all seriousness and said, "I know."

I had no idea where Peanut could have hidden the stuff. Knowing him, he'd have left a sign. Benjie knew the system of chalk marks and sigils we used as well as I did and we both searched but there was nothing.

"Peanut knows you," Benjie said finally. "Where would he have put it so you could find it?"

The last time I'd been with Peanut, we were on the roof. He'd banged twice on the vent up there and I'd thought he was just being dramatic like Peanut always was.

I looked at Benjie. He was looking at me like he knew I knew and he didn't know what else to say to make me trust him. I didn't know if I could or not but I didn't have much choice. "The roof," I said. "It's on the roof."

We climbed up there and stopped, staring. I hadn't had such a good view of the crash site since the last time we were up there.

"Holy shit," Benjie said. "They've got in."

UM had the whole crashed ship lit up in floodlights, gunships buzzing overhead, troops in powered armour clambering over it. We could hear a faint clanging clamour and buzz of heavy lifting, winching and cutting gear.

I sagged. I didn't know how much more stuffing could get knocked out of me. "Do you think they'll turn on the colony when they're done with the ship?" I said.

We both looked sideways, along the walls, to where the Imperial troops were stationed, watching, looking so much smaller, uncertain which way to even point their guns.

"I don't know," Benjie said. "Shit, Luka, is that what you're thinking? That the Wintrans are going to…?" He cut off what he was going to say, shaking his head.

I couldn't tell if he felt sorry for me or was pissed at me.

I shrugged. I had a lump in my throat. "Is Dayton working with them?"

He shook his head again and looked around. "Where do you reckon this stuff is?" He sounded tired.

I limped towards the vent and reached my hand into it, feeling around. There was something stuck in there with tape. I peeled it off and pulled it out. I knew from the shape and the weight of it that it was the tiny slick little access key I'd lifted from the IDC guy in black fatigues.

"We need to find out what's on this," I said, looking up.

Benjie had his rifle in his hands, casual but his finger on the trigger. "Shit," he said as if he'd been thinking that I'd been fooling around and now he could see it, he knew this was real. "Come on. I know someone who can help us."

We went back through the streets towards the fighting. I had the key stuffed deep inside my pocket, limping along but as hyped as I've ever been. Like I said, it's awesome what adrenaline can do for you. I could hardly feel the stabbing pain in my knee any more.

I kept my head down, hood up, but I was watching every angle ahead, listening to every sound from behind. No one came near us.

They had stockpiles of crates at every corner, vehicles offloading weapons, rocket launchers, heavy machine guns. I gawped at it all. There was no way they'd take down the garrison but they were going to have a damn good try. It should have been exciting, exhilarating, but it felt wrong. It all felt wrong and I had no idea why.

I limped after Benjie, becoming slowly aware of a deep rumbling behind us, the ground trembling. I turned. He grabbed my shoulder and steered me towards an alleyway. I resisted, twisting around, looking behind us. I wanted to see what it was.

A chill dread was twisting in my stomach. Even in the darkness, I knew what it was before it appeared, a massive hulking shape, filling the street, three stories high, even bigger than a DZ. It was trundling on huge tracks, making the ground shake. They must have hacked its AI. It was surrounded by KRM fighters who were leading it like it was a lumbering prisoner of war.

Benjie pulled me close and slapped his hand against my back. "We're going to take down the garrison and you gave us the way in, squirt. We're going to break down their damn walls with their own damn robot."

He pushed me ahead of him into the narrow alley. The KRM didn't have any heavy weapons, no tanks or artillery, but I'd given them the perfect means to breach the walls. I glanced back. It was bristling with crushing rams and mining lasers and could blast its way through a mountain. It wasn't built for combat, and as long as the garrison's automated defences held, it shouldn't be able to get near but if the resistance could take out the weapons platforms, it would make short work of the walls. I felt sick. Benjie laughed and nudged me forward.

He led me through the alley and into the old market square. People were huddled around braziers, flickering lights dancing in the dark interiors of at least half the empty shops. They saw us but they didn't approach. Benjie walked with purpose, casual but confident, and I was just a brazen kid trooping along after him. He headed down another alleyway and my heart rate increased a notch, if that was possible.

Benjie stopped, glanced back at me and stepped aside. "After you," he breathed and gestured towards a doorway, door half ajar, a faint glow of light coming from inside.

Every instinct was screaming at me to run but I wasn't about to ditch out then, not after everything that had happened. I nodded and went past, took a deep breath and stepped inside. Benjie was right behind me. I almost hesitated. There was a tug at my hood as it was pulled down and a nudge in my back that sent me stumbling forwards.

I caught my balance, a curse on the tip of my tongue, but I looked up and saw Dayton sitting there, facing the door, looking right at me, gun in hand, Maisie sitting bolt upright in a chair next to him, a rag tied around her mouth, wrists taped together, and my entire world spun on its heels.

So much for my amazing intuition.

20

Dayton was perched on a desk, looking more like an underworld criminal boss than a resistance leader. Maybe that's what he had been the whole time.

Benjie pushed me forwards again.

I shrugged him off with a glare. He closed the door behind him and stood to one side.

I stood there, frozen like a total idiot, looking from him to Dayton.

Dayton stood, raising the gun and shaking his head with some kind of twisted wry smile like he was amazed I could be so stupid.

I was amazed I could have been so stupid.

"He's got it," Benjie said, even sounding different. "He doesn't know what's on it. I told you I could get him for you." He grinned at me. "Hey, nothing personal, squirt, it's just business."

I took a step back, not sure I'd heard right. Benjie was looking to Dayton for approval, nothing left of the kid I'd looked up to, admired, freaking wanted to be most of my life. It suddenly dawned on me with a sickening clarity that Maisie had been right all along. Benjie had used me, he'd always used me, as he'd got older and more cautious he'd sent me into places that were too risky for him…

"giving you the benefit of my experience," and, "helping you get better," he'd said. Ironically, that's exactly what had happened, but I realised then, it wasn't out of any sense of brotherhood or caring for my benefit but always to further his own ends. I felt sick when I thought how it was him who'd sent us out to the processing plant, how I'd disabled the security system, just so they could get in there?

Benjie spoke again, rubbing his hands together. "Okay, Dayton, I've kept my end of the bargain, now where's my payment?"

Dayton nodded, slow and deliberate. "Well done, Benjamin," he said. "You've earned exactly what's coming to you." And he switched aim so fast I almost missed the look on Benjie's face as he realised what was happening. The silenced bullet was in the air before he could open his mouth to object.

It hit.

He dropped without a sound.

I didn't understand at first why Dayton didn't shoot me too and I was half a heartbeat from turning and running except Maisie was still staring at me, something almost like an apology in her eyes.

Benjie's rifle was on the floor. I reckoned I could reach it. I shifted my weight slightly. I didn't want my knee to give out.

Dayton laughed. "Don't do it, kid. Come on, look at what we have here. That key you have? You're going to do a job for me. You've caused me quite a problem stealing that so I'd like you to take it back. Right now. Or I will kill your little girlfriend here and then I will kill your grandmother, slowly."

I must have scowled because he smiled and added, "I'll bet an old girl like that won't last too long though, hey? Do we have an understanding here?"

Another booming clamour reverberated in from the darkness where UM were tearing apart the crashed ship that had started all this. I used to think too much, about what had caused this, what had caused that, what if I had done something, what if I hadn't. In the end, you just get numb and stop caring.

I held up the tiny device.

Maisie was still staring at me.

"What is it?" I said.

My mind was running riot. Trojan or worm virus, I reckoned, something to screw up the base so they could attack it. But I'd stolen it from an Earth guy. He'd had IDC insignia on his uniform but he could have been anyone. He could have been a UM plant or some guy Dayton had brought in. I couldn't believe I'd been so naïve and so stupid as to pick his pocket when I had no idea who he was. If Charlie hadn't spotted me as I was running away from the garrison, I wouldn't even have been in there to run into him.

Dayton leaned back casually against the desk, the gun resting against his thigh, that smug smirk still on his face. "You don't need to know what it is."

"The guy I stole this from, was he UM?"

He laughed again. "You're not as smart as you think, kid. Now, you want what's left of your little family to survive this, then you are going to take that key back to the garrison and find a way to get it into a secure terminal. Do you understand?"

I shook my head. "That's impossible."

Dayton was looking at me as if he was reading my soul. "You're telling me you can't do it?"

He might as well have called me out on a dare and waved a red rag. He glanced at Maisie as if to remind me what was at stake. I had no choice anyway. He was threatening the two people who mattered the most to me in my entire world. The only people I cared about that I had left.

I stared back at him. "I can't hack a secure terminal without the AI triggering an alarm."

"Kid, I'm not telling you to hack it," he said, looking at me as if I was really slow. "Find a way in then just get that access key to a secure terminal inside the garrison."

"Then what?"

He tossed across another key.

"Use this. Just get it in there. It'll do what it has to once it's connected."

"I'll need help," I said without thinking. "There are two security protocols you have to bust to get in. You need to nullify two nodes to get access. I can't get them both at the same time. They're in different areas of the garrison. Give me Maisie and we'll get in there and fix it. And then you let us go and you let Latia go."

"You're not in any position to negotiate, kid," he said. He must have picked up on the desperation in my voice and he called my bluff. "Find a way in. You have six hours." He walked forward and retrieved Benjie's rifle without turning his back on me. I don't know what he thought I might do. "And trust me," he added, "you talk to anyone, tamper with it, or try anything, I will know, and I can make life really unpleasant for little Maisie here and grandma. You understand?" He looked at me with disdain. "You know the telecoms tower out by the ore plant? You want to see them alive again, then do what I've said and meet me there with those keys. In six hours. Now go. Scram. Don't let these lovely ladies down now."

I looked at Maisie.

She must have felt that I was about to do something stupid because she shook her head ever so slightly, eyes wide.

"Can I at least say goodbye?" I asked, belligerently.

Dayton waved the gun at me casually. "Sure, kid, it's your time that's wasting."

I walked over to Maisie, gently pulled the rag away from her mouth and leaned in. She didn't speak, just looked at me with fear and pleading in her eyes and shook her head again.

I whispered quietly, "Don't worry, it's going to be okay. I'm going to get us out of here. All of us." I kissed her then and before Dayton could react, I snapped Charlie's band off my wrist and on to Maisie's.

Dayton jumped up and shouted, pointing the gun at me but I knew he wouldn't shoot.

I spun and stared him down. He needed me and we both knew it. What he didn't need was Maisie and as soon as I walked out of the door chances were that he'd put a bullet in her head.

"What the hell is that?" he said.

"Life signs monitor," I said, cocky as hell. "Live feed tracking system. It's one I stole and we've hacked it so we can monitor it."

The look on Dayton's face darkened as the implications of what I'd just done started to dawn on him but I figured I'd spell it out for him anyway. "I have someone tracking this. If it gets taken off, I'll know. If she dies, I'll know. Either way, you get nothing."

Dayton wasn't stupid but he wasn't a poker player either. Bluff and counter bluff. Like I said, Charlie taught me a lot that night in the storm.

"Fine," Dayton growled. "Looks like we have ourselves a standoff, kid. Maybe I misjudged you after all, but understand this, I'm on a clock here which means this is a time limited offer. If I don't have those keys back in my hand in six hours, she dies regardless. You understand?"

"Six hours and counting." I turned and walked out.

I didn't look round and Dayton didn't shoot me in the back. I kept to the shadows. The sound of gunfire was increasing in all directions. Someone had set fire to a jeep on the main road north. There were other fires burning all over the southern part of the city, buildings alight, cars overturned, barricades in flames. It didn't feel real, like I was walking through some kind of hellish nightmare. Like I might wake up at any minute in Latia's house, with no pain, just her ragging on me for not going to school and calling me down for pancakes.

I had a horrible feeling she wasn't alright. That Dayton had lied and she was dead already, but that was something I had no control over so I just had to hope she was okay, trying to figure out instead what had happened with Benjie while trying to watch out for trouble, working a route through.

I headed north, flinching back every time I heard voices too close. It seemed like the whole city was burning. My knee had stiffened up again and I was riding the pain with each step, even with the crutches. I took it easy, slinking my way through the shadows, past Dayton's guys and past the fighting. They were pushing up close to the garrison at my favourite spot. I could hear kids' voices in amongst the fevered shouting, higher pitched yells screaming over the gunfire, as if it was a game.

I watched for a while from the shadows of an alleyway, despair setting in as I realised there was no way in.

I wanted to get into the garrison and I wanted it so badly that it became my whole world, each step, each breath, each heartbeat, each pulse of adrenaline. The fight flowed around me as if it was orchestrated in slow motion. Earth, the resistance, UM. None of them mattered. All I wanted was to get in there and click that key into place to see what was on it, see what was so important that it was getting the people I cared about killed.

But there was no way in. The Earth troops were pulling back, tanks and APCs withdrawing into the garrison, every soldier they had manning heavy weapon placements and sniper positions around the wall, bolstering the automated AI defence grid. They were preparing for a siege. There was no way I could get across there without getting shot.

I didn't know what to do.

There was no way I could even get to the wall, never mind over it and into the complex. UM were crawling over our desert and the KRM had the mines, the refinery, half the city and soon, they'd have the garrison and the space port.

I was paralysed by indecision. First time in my life. And it terrified me. I'd always been so damn cocky, so sure of myself. I always had an answer. I could always see the patterns, the way in, the way out, the solution to the problem. But in that chaos, there was no pattern. Panic started to set in, fear of failure, fear of losing Latia and Maisie. If anyone ever tells you I'm never scared of anything, it's not true, I just don't let it get to me. I thought I'd burned all the scared out of me as a five year old when I was trapped in the rubble that had been my home.

But that night, it flooded back and, with it, I flashed back to a memory of another time, something Charlie had once said to me… "You freeze, you die. Make a decision. Act. Deal with the consequences later, and believe me, there will always be consequences, but in the moment you have to do something. Right or wrong. Good or bad. But do something." So I did something, something I'd never done before because I hated the idea of doing it. Something I was maybe even afraid of and the thought of needing to do it made me feel dreadful. I decided to ask someone for help.

If the southern part of the city was in chaos, the north was in meltdown. Sirens were wailing, smoke spiralling from buildings hit by rockets the KRM had launched at targets further north. Another hit as I headed across Tenth, some way off but close enough to make the ground tremble. I had my hood up, head down, taking one step after another, every muscle complaining. The streets up there were usually deserted under curfew. That night, as the city sparked and burned, they swarmed. It was like someone had hit the panic button and they couldn't get away fast enough.

I joined the throng of people edging between the cars and trucks that were trying to get to the space port, expecting someone to tug at my collar any minute and expose me, yell at me that I wasn't their kind, that I wasn't welcome or worthy to share in their moment of terror as the troubles from the south impinged on their privileged lives. I was jostled, swept along, but no one called me out.

There were no troops on the streets and as we got closer to the perimeter of the landing field, I could see why. They'd reinforced the patrols and set up an outer ring of defences, tanks and APCs set up back to back with gun turrets pointed outwards towards the growing crowds of colonists trying frantically to evacuate. There was no way I was going to make it over the fence like I usually did. I worked my way round and pushed through until I could see the gate. The soldiers were checking passes, documents, scanning those nice folk with implants, searching every car. Those with the right permits, right clearance, the right birth certificates were being waved through, those without were being firmly turned away.

I sucked in a deep breath. I knew Peanut had to be in there, I just needed to get to him. I watched the soldiers shout brusquely, push anyone who wasn't cooperating fast enough, armed guards on high alert hefting rifles.

The darkness and despair started to creep back.

There was no way in.

21

You remember what I said about luck? Sometimes you can have the best hand and you know you're on a winner, sometimes you just need the right card to drop for you. And sometimes you just need to be in the right place at the right time. Fate is funny that way, she can bite you on the ass or throw you a bone.

I started to turn away. I almost didn't hear the high-pitched squeal, someone yelling my name and louder shouts to get back. I looked up. Spacey was running full tilt at me, adults running after her, shouting, one of them the schoolteacher from the outpost, her face fraught and drawn. Spacey bowled into me and hugged tight, her arms wrapped around my leg. I forgot I still had the stupid war paint on my face and looked up as the adults approached.

They slowed, looking horrified. They reached out an arm towards Spacey as if they needed to coax her away from me. She nuzzled deeper, sobbing, crying that she wanted to stay with me, that she wanted me to go with them, crying for Maisie and screaming louder when they inched forward and tried to take her arm.

I couldn't get her off me. Short of flinging her away, I couldn't get her to let go. A gunship roared overhead. She screamed louder. One of the adults, a guy who looked like he was probably a teacher too, that or some kind of social worker, put up his hands like he was going to try to negotiate with me or something. Like I was some kind of dangerous resistance fighter threatening their escape. It's a good thing I didn't have a gun. That would have freaked them out even more.

The schoolteacher squinted at me and swore. "No, wait," she said, putting her hands up as if she was trying to calm it all down. I don't know what they thought I was going to do. She stepped forward, glancing back at the guy and saying, "I know this kid." She looked at me again. "Luka? It's Luka, isn't it? Is that right?"

I don't even know what I did. Probably scowled at her.

She turned back to the guy. "We have to take him. He's one of the street kids that we registered for the school. He's coming with us. Come on, both of you. We have to get back in line."

I went with them, Spacey clinging to me. They led us through the crowd to a school bus that was inching forward in a line of other vehicles. The schoolteacher urged us to climb on board and steered us to a seat at the front. It was packed with other kids who all stared at me. I felt like I was from another planet. I held onto Spacey and stared out of the window. The soldiers at the gate were getting more and more agitated as the crowd pressed. They stopped the bus, yelled and hammered on the door to get it opened. The kids were whispering and whimpering to each other. I wanted to be anywhere but on that bus.

One of the soldiers climbed in, rifle in his arms, corporal's stripes on his uniform. My heart was going nineteen to the dozen. I could smell the smoke and explosive fumes on my clothes. He looked round at us all, his eye catching mine for a second. I stared back, blank, bracing myself, expecting to be hauled off there and then and shot as KRM, but he just turned to the driver and said, "Only adults with current visas. The kids are all native. They stay."

There was a clamour, crying. Spacey gripped my hand tight. I shifted my weight to get up but the schoolteacher stepped forward. "No, we all go. We have papers for all these children."

They didn't have papers for me. The school had given me some when they made me enrol but I'd lost those years ago.

She was steadfastly avoiding looking at me.

The corporal shook his head. "We have orders. Transport is limited. We're taking citizens with visas. With somewhere to go. The adults can go through. This bus needs to back the hell up."

He turned. She stepped in front of him and he shoved her aside. There were more yells. I stood, shaking off Spacey's hand and standing in front of her. The soldier went to bring up his rifle. In a bus full of schoolchildren, he went to raise his rifle. The driver was shouting, the other adults were shouting, the schoolteacher the loudest, and it felt like the guy was a hair's breadth from opening fire but another soldier climbed on board, hands up, yelling for quiet, telling his buddy to stand down, for Christ's sake. "We've got a transport," he said. "Freighter captain just in from Erica says he'll ditch his cargo and take the kids. Corporal, get them all processed and get them through. Christ, this is the last thing we need."

He left.

The corporal was pissed and started demanding papers. The schoolteacher turned to me. She mouthed, "Sit down," trying to be reassuring but her hands were shaking.

I sat. Spacey clambered onto my lap and we sat there as the school staff fumbled out all the official crap they had to appease the asshole corporal. I had no idea how she accounted for me. I perched on that seat as the bus finally pulled through the gate and into the port, heart pounding, injured leg stretched out, Spacey sitting on my other knee, and it would have been so easy to go with it, just close my eyes and go with them.

But it could never be that easy.

The bus pulled up at some kind of terminal building and they ferried us off and inside. I hesitated at the door. I held Spacey's hand tight and leaned down to whisper in her ear. The woman was watching us. Spacey did me proud. She listened intently to every word I said. I felt her little chin go up, that defiance we had ingrained into us kicking in.

"I'll come find you," I whispered. "I promise."

She hugged me tighter.

I stood up. "I need the bathroom," I said.

The schoolteacher looked at me, something like dismay in her eyes. She nodded, took Spacey's hand and led her away.

I split.

We were inside the perimeter. All the attention was focused outwards, inside no one was watching too closely. I checked the time and limped out across to the workshops.

The maintenance bays were open, seemingly abandoned. There was the small courier ship Peanut had mentioned and a couple of shuttles parked up in the service bays. But there were no people in sight and it was obvious Peanut wasn't there. I wondered if he'd found a way off-world already, if he was even still alive, and my heart sank. I stood there in the dark, chest heaving, leaning heavily on the crutches.

He walked in behind me, flicked on the light and made me jump out of my skin.

"Comms are back," he said, throwing tools and components onto the workbench. He didn't even seem surprised to see me. "Whatever was on that ship jamming comms, UM must have trashed it when they got in. They're in, did you see that? And there's Imperial reinforcements inbound. They're less than a day out. The garrison can probably hold out that long, I reckon, then it's going to get really ugly."

I didn't care. I pulled the key out of my pocket and held it up. "You need to help me get this into the garrison,"

I said, words sticking in my throat. "Dayton's going to kill Maisie and Latia unless I do it and I can't get in." I faltered. That was still tough to admit. "Peanut…"

He wiped his hand on a rag. "That's the key you stole. I had a feeling that's why Dayton wanted you dead. I figured it had to be something to do with that."

I checked the time again. My hand was shaking. "He's had a change of heart. Seems he doesn't want me dead now. He needs me to do something for him. With this key, and I don't even know what it is. I have to get back into the garrison and get to a secure terminal. I have less than four hours or he's going to kill them… Peanut, I don't know how to get in."

"I tried to get back to you," he said. "What happened?"

I couldn't breathe and I opened my mouth to say Benjie the son of a bitch betrayed me but I couldn't say it. I shook my head. "Just tell me how I get in."

Standing in that workshop, with Dayton's people setting fire to our city and Imperial forces about to descend on the colony in force, I reckoned I'd just run at the wall if there was no other option. I'd figure something out or die trying. Latia and Maisie deserved that from me at least.

I was trembling, about to walk away and be damned when Peanut shrugged in that unassuming way of his and said simply, "You don't need to. That diplomatic vessel is still parked right outside. Get on board that and you have a connection right into the heart of the garrison."

I think I just stared at him but he was throwing me a lifeline.

"It's the only remote access into the whole secure level of the base," he said, throwing me a pair of maintenance crew overalls that were two sizes too big, and a pass that wouldn't fool anyone if they so much as glanced at it. "A diplomatic vessel will have all the security clearance you need. And it'll be a damn sight easier to break into than a garrison under siege."

I grabbed the overalls and struggled into them without thinking.

He looked me up and down and laughed. "Yeah, you look nothing like an engineer. Just keep your head down. And leave the crutches. I'll get you something that'll help."

Peanut also gave me a headset, a tiny bead to stick in my ear, and told me we could talk if needed but keep it to a minimum. I gave him a hand to throw a load of parts and kit into crates on a loader then hunkered down between them as he drove out. The whole place was still in chaos. I could hear the shouts and yells as the soldiers at the gate processed the incoming crowds. It was getting more and more desperate. Peanut drove round and stopped at the accident and emergency centre that was across from the terminal building. I stayed down and out of sight. He vanished inside and reappeared, tossing a small box to me and jumping back into the cab.

I braced myself as he drove off again, fumbling open the box and downing a handful of the painkillers, double dosing, not realising how bad it had got until it started to ease off. The drugs kicking in gave me a rush of confidence that started to push out the despair. I could do this. I was the kid that could do anything, who'd never been caught. I felt like I was holding all the aces and the game was mine to control.

Peanut drove the loader right up to the diplomatic ship. I hid there, listening as Peanut argued with the guards on the access ramp that he didn't care they didn't know they had a bust Prazi manifold, it had been reported and it was flashing up warnings on all systems, and if they wanted to make orbit before the space port was overrun they better let him on board to fix it. They bitched that no one had notified them but as Peanut pointed out, the whole place was in turmoil and the space port personnel were barely able to maintain what little order there was. It was hardly surprising in all the chaos, he said, that no one was telling anyone what was going on. I heard the guards grumble their agreement, the life of the military grunt, the other sagely conceding that it was not theirs to reason why. They laughed at that then told Peanut he'd better make it fast because they had clearance to go as soon as the boss got back.

While he distracted the guards, I dropped down and sneaked around the back of the loader and up the ramp. I glanced over my shoulder as Peanut got the guards to help him unload the heaviest crate. Then I was in.

The entry way was undoubtedly being scanned, but the guards on the ramp had just called in that maintenance technicians were coming on board for urgent repairs so I was banking on nobody watching a monitor being surprised at seeing a guy in coveralls coming on board. I paused for a moment to get my bearings, orienting from what I'd seen of the outside of the ship with what I expected inside. She was a big ship but not huge, not one of the deep spacers that hauled millions of tonnes of freight and cargo across space. There would be a flight deck, crew's quarters, a messing area, engine room and a secure communications area. That was where I needed to get to.

I ditched the baggy overalls behind some containers. I reckoned I'd have a better chance of pulling off dumb, scared kid trying to sneak off planet than I did maintenance engineer. I would even have squeezed out a tear or two if required. Most grown ups really don't know what to do with a hysterical kid. It makes them uncomfortable and I figured if it came to it and I blubbed enough, they'd be more likely to ditch me onto the terminal staff than arrest me for spying or terrorism.

I moved round the bay to an airlock that was open. I could see the cameras monitoring the bay. The two security guys were huffing and puffing up the loading ramp as they struggled with Peanut's overloaded crate.

I took a gamble that anyone watching was focused on them and I darted through the airlock into a corridor, instinctively turned right and saw what I was looking for. Maintenance access hatch. There was a maintenance terminal just inside. It wouldn't give me access to ship's systems without a pass key and I didn't have time to hack it, but I didn't need to, all I needed was the general layout of the ship's deck plans. They flashed up. A quick glance was all I needed then I split.

I went up and pulled myself into a cable conduit. It was tight but I'd been in worse and I wormed my way along until I reached a junction where there was an access to the ventilation system. No electrobes because there was no AI. Earth would never have an AI on one of their black ops ships. I popped open a grill and squeezed through a hole that was uncomfortably small, scraping skin and drawing blood as I went. It seemed like Lady Luck was dealing me another good card. In another six months time I wouldn't have been able to get through it at all.

The vent shaft was only slightly wider. No adult could ever have fitted through it. I wriggled as fast as I could, hoping I wasn't too late. I reached the spot I was after, directly above the comms centre. If it was manned, this all came to an end here but Fate dealt me another ace and the room was empty. I still couldn't enter though, not yet. I carefully removed the ventilation grill, being careful not to trigger the mesh of laser sensor beams across the opening. The conduit might not have been large enough for an adult to squeeze through but that didn't mean Earth wasn't paranoid enough or stupid enough to leave every opening into a secure area unprotected. I got into position. Now it was all down to Peanut.

After what seemed like an age had passed, and with my arms starting to scream and tremble with the strain of the braced position I was holding, the lights flickered off ever so briefly and that was my signal. As we'd planned, Peanut had killed the main power and disrupted the backup from kicking in.

I heard him say, "Go," over the headset and I moved. It gave me only seconds before the power was back on. I dropped through the small hole. I wish I could say it was impressive, that I performed some amazing feat of acrobatics and flipped to land on my feet with feline-like grace. The truth was that I fell like a bag of rocks, hit a console, bounced off, crashed into a chair and cracked my head for good measure. Everything went hazy for a second then I looked up. The lights were back on, the detection grid was functional again, there was a trickle of blood running into my eye but there were no alarms going off. And there was a secure Imperial Diplomatic Corps communications terminal right in front of me.

I pulled the access key out of my pocket, stuck it into the terminal and watched as it came to life, scrolling numbers and accessing systems so fast it was dizzying.

I don't know what I was expecting but I was past caring. I just wanted it done. It slowed and started to process a series of protocols. And that's when it got my attention.

It wasn't even accessing the garrison's database. It was all right there on the ship. I watched as it ran through reports and configured accounts. It didn't take much to add it all up.

"Oh shit," I whispered, heart sinking and a chill descending so fast I shivered.

Peanut suddenly sounded loud in my ear. I'd forgotten I was even wearing the comms gear. "How's it going, squirt? I'm pretty much finished here. I've tinkered with some stuff and changed out a few parts but these goons are looking over my shoulder. I can bluff them but they're going to start getting twitchy if I take much longer. How are you doing?"

I didn't know what to say.

"Luka?"

"Peanut, it's a ledger." I grabbed at the terminal, fingers twitching, shoulders trembling. I got it to respond and I got it to do what I wanted. I started to query it, pulling up stats and reports, feeling sick deep inside as I saw what had been going on.

"A ledger?" he said across the connection. "Why would Dayton want you killed over a ledger? That doesn't make sense, does it?"

"None of it does." I couldn't say what was going through my head.

I hesitated.

"What's wrong?"

"Dayton gave me another key."

"Put it in."

I had a really bad feeling, deep inside, tugging at every instinct I had.

Peanut nudged me. "Do it."

I pulled it out of my pocket and stuck it into the terminal, watching as it engaged and half expecting there to be a bang, a massive boom as the garrison exploded.

It didn't. The terminal started to scroll through the ledger. Numbers flashed up as it accessed an account and began transferring tens of millions of Imperial credits.

The connection engaged again. "What the hell is it doing?" Peanut said.

"It's making Dayton rich," I muttered.

"What?"

"Dayton's not working for the resistance, he's working for the Empire."

22

I sat back, watching as the money flowed. "They've been paying him. They've been paying him to betray us and keep the rebellion as ineffective as hell. That's why he wanted me. He thought I knew. That's why he needed me dead." It caught in my throat as I said it. "So I couldn't tell anyone. You should see this."

I pulled up one report after another.

"He's been working with them the whole time." I scrolled back and paused the stats. "That offensive two years ago, when they tried to clear us out… we took massive losses, the Imperial forces took nothing." I scrolled back again. "That time Dayton blew the supply lines to the mines…" I almost laughed, "…it was staged. They knew exactly where and when he was going to attack and had countermeasures in place before he even instigated it. When Dayton attacked the airfield, the trucks they destroyed were obsolete. They were left there for him to destroy. So it could look like a victory." I sat there staring at it. "The Earth forces didn't lose anything. It was all staged… It goes right back."

"To Rainfall?"

I had a lump in my throat. "Yeah, Dayton told them where we were."

Where the leaders of the resistance were. It wasn't by chance that our building, that my family was targeted. It was a surgical strike.

And the whole time the numbers flashed and the cash flowed into Dayton's account.

It finished and I thought that was going to be it, but then it started to transfer data, lists and names, account numbers, downloading the full details of the ledger from the IDC database onto Dayton's key. It was a whole list of people on the Empire's payroll. And not just on Kheris.

"We can't let him get away with it," Peanut said through the link.

"No."

There was a clatter and brief static.

Peanut cursed. "Whatever you have to do," he sent, "do it fast."

I heard him yelling at whoever had come in, banging something and complaining loudly that their coupling system was shot as well.

I looked back at the terminal and the data scrolling across it. I'd only got a glance but I knew every line of that ledger, each digit of every account on it, every detail of every transaction. I knew enough to sink Dayton forever. I just had to decide what to do with it. And then I realised something. The key hadn't just opened the data file, the account it was transferring funds to was an Imperial account. The type that every Imperial citizen is given at birth.

I reached for the terminal.

Peanut yelled to them that he was finished before I was done. My hand was shaking so bad I almost blew it. I hit the last command, pulled out the keys and abandoned the terminal. Peanut told me to run so I ran.

The ship was firing up its engines before we even got back to the workshops.

Peanut shoved me inside. "What now?"

"We need to get away." I emptied the box of painkillers, trying to figure out how many more I could take. "I need to go get Maisie and Latia and we need to get out of here."

He squinted at me. Peanut knew me too well. And he'd never questioned me, never chided me, never doubted me. And right then, he said, "What have you done?" like for the first time, he wasn't sure.

I looked up at him. "Can you get that courier ready to fly?"

He knew exactly what I was talking about. "You're not seriously thinking you can fly it?"

"I can fly it. I know I can."

"Luka, reading a manual and playing kid's games in a burned out wreck isn't the same as being able to fly one. Knowing what to do isn't the same as knowing how to do it."

"Do you have a better idea?"

He cursed. "How long have I got?"

"Two hours. I'll get them back here. You get it ready to fly."

"Two hours?"

I downed the last of the drugs. "Peanut, the resistance are going to realise they can't take the garrison so they'll try to take the port. We have to get out of here."

He looked at me and nodded slowly. "You're going to take on Dayton?"

"I'm going to get Maisie and Latia. Be ready when we get back."

He didn't look convinced.

Getting out of the space port was easier than getting in. Peanut loaded up a truck and drove me out. The soldiers on the gate were pissed off and hassled, the pressing throng getting desperate as the number of rockets hitting the north increased and the gunfire got closer. Peanut showed his papers and drove right through, revving the engine to clear the way. He stopped in a side street next to a load of abandoned vehicles, and leaned through the window as I started trying car door handles. "How are you going to get back in?"

I tried the ignition on a bike. It fired up. "I'll find a way," I said and gave him a grin as I climbed onto it. "Just get that ship ready."

I went through the maze of narrow streets, gunning it back across Main as fast as I could. I didn't turn on the lights and I didn't slow as I took the corners, skidding and almost losing it a couple of times, riding around burning barricades and blockades. I was heading away from the trouble, not towards it, so no one was too concerned with me, at least no one shot at me and I made it to the outskirts with less than half an hour to make it out to the tower.

It was a powerful bike, heavier than the dirt bikes I was used to, and it was fast. There's no way I would have made it otherwise. I rode across the desert, the city in flames behind me, UM vessels filling the sky around the crashed ship ahead of me. They were withdrawing, abandoning it. Gunships were buzzing round it in circles like vultures. They were wrapping up and clearing the vicinity. If they turned on the city, we were done. I opened the throttle and floored it, wheels spinning in the dust as I threw it into turns to avoid boulders and craters on the desert floor. I couldn't feel my knee. I couldn't feel anything. I could see the tower up ahead, didn't waste time checking how long I had left and skidded up in a cloud next to the ramshackle building.

It was dark, only glances of moonlight and occasional searchlight beams shimmering off the broken windows.

I cut the engine and sat there, blinking dust out of my eyes, adrenaline pounding through my chest, almost thinking I'd imagined the whole thing, got the instructions wrong or something, but then Dayton stepped out and stood there looking at me.

I got off the bike and limped forward.

Another figure emerged behind Dayton. Calum, I could recognise him anywhere. He was holding the damn rifle.

They stared at me.

I couldn't see Maisie or Latia anywhere.

"You made it," Dayton called out. He held out his hands. "Well done, kid. Now where are my keys?"

"Where's Maisie?" I yelled back.

"The keys," he shouted. He turned to Calum and said something.

Calum sloped off. Even in the low light, I could see the smirk on his face.

Dayton stepped forward, beckoning with his hand. "The keys."

I shook my head slowly. "I know what you've been doing."

"Kid, you have no idea what I'm doing. Now hand over the keys and scram."

I took a step forward. "I do know."

He did a double take, screwed up his face and glared at me. "What?" He walked at me, towering over me, close up, grabbing my shirt and shoving me in the chest. "You know nothing, boy. Where are my keys?"

I twisted away and backed off, keeping my left hand behind my back.

"I've seen all the records," I said. "I know what you've been doing."

I blurted it all out, faster and faster, backing away from him and spilling everything I knew about the betrayals, the attacks, the set ups.

The look on his face got even darker, that muscle ticking in the side of his jaw. He was keeping pace with me, one step at a time.

"I know about Rainfall," I said, keeping my chin up and

my weight mostly on my right leg. "I know you sold us out." I felt so cold, even saying it out loud didn't spark any of the emotion I'd always been hit with even thinking of that night. "You told them where we'd be, exactly where we were, Dayton. You told them where to drop those bombs."

I took another step back, glancing aside as a moving cloud of dust caught my eye. There was a vehicle approaching from the foothills, not the city. No lights but it was moving fast. And it was coming straight for us.

"Who the hell are they?" I said, incredulous, full flow. "You selling us out to UM now as well?"

Dayton laughed. "You don't know anything, kid. Now hand over the keys."

For all I knew, Calum could have had me in the sights of his rifle. They didn't need me alive. I backed off again, shaking my head, as the Wintran vehicle pulled up, engine purring. It was a jeep, flash corporate militia, fully armoured, glistening in the moonlight. I'd never seen a car that new and shiny, never been so close to that much money before.

The suit that stepped out was just as flash. The two bodyguards with him were wearing night vision goggles, stubby automatic rifles cradled in their arms. The main man walked forward.

Dayton suddenly looked really small.

"I trust you have the intel," the UM suit said, clipped words, but loud and clear.

I felt even smaller.

"Yes, I have," Dayton growled, "or at least I will as soon as I get it off this little shit."

"Are you telling me the child has it? Perhaps I should be dealing with him."

I might have laughed. That didn't go down well.

The suit looked at me. "Do you have it?"

The keys were weighing heavy in my pocket but I shook my head.

"Then we don't have a deal." He turned to walk away.

"Wait," Dayton said. His voice was shaking. "You have to take me with you. I can pay. Whatever you want." He didn't exactly drop to his knees to beg but he might as well have done. "I have money. You have to take me. They'll kill me if you leave me here."

The suit didn't even look back. "We have no need of money, Mr Dayton. Good luck with your rebellion."

He got into the jeep, the heavies with the guns got in behind him and they drove off.

Dayton was left standing staring after them, mouth open. He turned on me. "You little shit. You little Imperial bastard."

I grinned at him. "I transferred your millions," I said.

Dayton frowned. "I know. You think I'm stupid? That's what you were supposed to do. Who needs the damned Wintrans, anyway?"

"I transferred them to Maisie," I said quickly.

He stopped. "What?"

"All of it," I said. "Everything from your account, I transferred it to her."

Dayton stared at me open mouthed.

"Everything," I said. "All of it."

He grabbed at the holster.

I brought round my left hand and levelled his own gun at him. "Looking for this?"

He glowered at me.

I was holding the gun in two hands, looking down the barrel at him, and all the hurt, all the pain and intensity of every loss I'd ever felt focused into sharp clarity. I wanted to kill him for what he'd done to Maisie, to Latia, to Freddie, to Charlie, even Calum. I wanted him to die for what he'd done to us eight years ago on the night of Rainfall, and I wanted him to die knowing that he'd failed. That ultimately, he'd failed.

I wanted it to end.

I pulled the trigger.

The hammer fell with a hollow click. Misfire.

Dayton bellowed and ran at me.

I threw the gun at him and dodged, not well, the painkillers were wearing off and my knee was starting to scream at me again.

He caught me with a sideways backhanded blow and sent me sprawling. He reached behind his back and pulled out another gun.

I lay there, staring at him, staring at this son of a bitch who had sold us out, as he pointed the gun at me, and I laughed. "You've lost, Dayton," I said. "I took all your money and, you know what? The whole resistance will find out that you've been betraying them."

It wasn't the smartest thing I've ever done but I didn't care. Dayton's face was stone as he stepped forward. He steadied his aim and pulled the trigger.

23

There was a sharp crack. And another. I recoiled, jerked backwards, but it wasn't me that was hit. Dayton's bullet went wide, kicked into the dust beside me.

He staggered backwards, blood blossoming out across his chest. He tried to say something but he was choking, red spilling from his mouth. He crumpled and fell to the dirt.

I staggered to my feet and turned.

Calum emerged from the shadow of the building, a rifle held steady in his arms. He walked forward, stare not leaving Dayton's prone form, lying there on the ground, bleeding red into the dust.

I looked at him. "You heard all that?"

Calum nodded without taking his eyes off Dayton.

"I didn't betray anyone," I said.

"I know." He looked at me then, lowering the rifle. "Was that true about the money?"

"All of it."

Calum was fidgeting with the mechanism on the rifle and looked up again. "So Rainfall, that was him?"

He'd heard everything. Calum had lost family that night too. I wasn't the only one.

I nodded.

His expression didn't change. "Go. Luka, if you have a chance to go, go. Get the hell out of here." He glanced beyond me, finger stroking over the trigger. "The rebellion isn't over. And you don't want to be here when we take our chances next time."

He suddenly seemed really old.

Way older than I ever felt I could be.

"I'm not going without Maisie and Latia," I said.

He looked back at me and sucked in a deep breath. "I can take you to Latia." He hesitated, never a big one with words, but it was like he couldn't say what he was about to.

It felt like I'd been hit by a truck. I had ice in my stomach as I said, "Where's Maisie?"

He shook his head, overly solemn as ever. I knew he was going to say she was dead. I almost heard the words before he opened his mouth but instead he said, "She got captured."

"Captured?"

"She kicked Dayton in the nuts. Can you believe it? He was trying to bring her back, they ran into a patrol and she kicked him in the nuts." He forced a laugh. "She made a break for it and ran right to them. They took her into the garrison. We heard they're shipping out prisoners to be processed as war criminals."

I almost said, "We're kids, they can't do that to us." But we were carrying guns and wearing body armour, and we weren't throwing stones at them any more, we were throwing grenades. They could do what they wanted.

"Show me where Latia is," I said, "then I'll go get Maisie."

He took me to the tunnels. They were deserted, everyone out on the streets, fighting, pushing for the garrison. Wherever they were controlling it from, it wasn't Dayton's command bunker. We walked past that. The door was open. No guards. I couldn't help looking in. The guy with the black wristband, the one who'd given me the puzzles, was lying on the floor, a hole in his forehead. Two other guys were sprawled next to him, blood pooling.

Calum stopped. "He shot them."

I stood next to him, staring. "Who did?"

"Dayton. Just before we took off. He said they were traitors." He shook his head. "I guess they knew what was on the key. If it hadn't been for you, that's how I'd have ended up." He shivered.

I didn't have time for all this. "Calum, where's Latia?"

He turned away and led me down a side tunnel I'd never seen before, living quarters, cold and damp as hell.

"They've been looking after her," he said. "We've all been looking after her."

She was a Cole. Of course the resistance would look after her, whatever they thought I'd done. My great-grandfather had been one of its founding members so Latia was regarded almost as royalty.

It didn't make me feel any better.

He gestured towards a door, pulled back the bolt and stood aside to let me in.

Latia rose to her feet, cautiously as if she wasn't sure it was me. She looked tired but determined, a smile creasing her face as she stepped forward, arms outstretched.

She held me tight, then at arm's length, checking me over. "They've hurt you," she said, frowning.

Calum backed away, awkward. Damn right he should feel awkward.

"I'm fine," I muttered. "Come on, we have to leave. I have a way out. We're all going."

"I'm going home," she said in that tone you didn't ever argue with.

I shook my head. "You need to come with me. I'm going to get Maisie then we're going to get away from here."

She sat back down, still holding onto my hand, patting the seat next to her. I sat, struggling to hide the discomfort as pain shot up and down my leg.

She frowned again, looking at me intently, wiping a smudge off my face like I was tiny again. I was filthy, it was going to take more than that. She smiled. "Luka, this is my home. My family are here. All of my family are here. And they always will be. I'm a Kheris girl. This planet is in my blood. And I'm staying. You may have been born here, Luka, but you don't belong here."

I opened my mouth to object but she hushed me like she always used to, so soft it made everything okay.

"I'm old. I'm content here," she said. "This is not your future. You're special, Luka. You've always been special. And it's time for you to go." She reached into her pocket and pulled out the knotted bracelet, tying it back around my wrist. "Go and find Maisie, and go find your place in this galaxy that is so much more than this little corner we were born into."

I managed to whisper, "No."

She held her hand over my wrist. I could feel the heat from her skin, the heat from the stones knotted into the band. "I have other little ones to look after." She smiled again, warmth in her eyes. "And you have places to go."

My eyes were watering. It must have been the fumes down there.

"Go," she said softly. "Go… this is not where you belong now."

I'd said the exact same thing to Spacey.

Latia squeezed my hand. "Now," she said, sprightly, "let's go and see what state the house is in, shall we?"

Calum helped me get her there. I didn't stick around. I hugged her, told Calum he'd better take care of her then I left.

I don't know how I made it back up to the garrison but I made it to the corner and stood, looking left and right, breathing in the cool smoke-tinged air of that insane night, then walked across Main, out in the open, head up, the entire universe revolving around me as if it couldn't touch me. As if nothing could ever touch me again. All the clamour and noise seemed distant, muted. It was like I was daring someone to see me, challenging a bullet to even try to come close. One step after the next. The dark shadow of the rubble barrier loomed in front of me, higher than it had ever seemed before, more ominous, more threatening. It became the barrier that had stood in my way my whole life. I didn't belong in there and I didn't belong out here.

I started to run. Sound crashed back in, explosions deafeningly close, the sharp ping and retort of gunfire echoing past my ears. The pain in my knee became an all-encompassing focus of every hurt and loss I'd ever felt. It's amazing what you can do when you channel that intense need into energy.

A rocket hit the street behind me as I hit the barrier. I shielded my head from the cloud of dust and debris, coughing as I clambered up and over, sliding down the other side and hunkering down in its shadow.

The open killing ground between the barrier and the wall was hectic, more alive than I'd ever seen it.

There was a flurry of movement, shouting and yells to reinforce the west wall, a roar of engines as they geared up to move round. I braced myself to move. I could only think of one way in. It was too obvious. I pushed back my hood and scrubbed my sleeve across my face, trying to rub off the black paint. I wasn't part of the resistance any more and I didn't want it to look like I was.

I struggled to my feet and staggered around the edge of the killing ground, keeping close to the rubble until I reached the main approach then cut out into the open and straight in towards the gatehouse. I must have looked pathetic. With every step, I was expecting someone to spot me and open fire. It didn't take long. They didn't shoot me but they came out, rifles up, screaming at me to stop. I put my hands up in surrender, stumbled on something and went down to one knee, the other giving out completely.

I was surrounded fast. They could see I was a kid and I had no weapons but they still grabbed my hands and slapped cuffs tight around my wrists. Someone was shouting that they should check me for goddamned bombs. Someone else pulled me up, fingers digging hard into my shoulder, and shoved me forward with a punch to the back of my head. I almost went down again but someone else stepped in, the sergeant who had given me Charlie's stuff, and he grabbed me and propelled me forward, yelling to the others, "Stand down, it's Anderton's kid. Get him inside."

And just like that, I was escorted into the garrison.

The sergeant was arguing with the others as they took me in. I didn't even know his name. He fended them off and walked me past a holding room where there were a couple of KRM hard men, in cuffs, looking sullen, staring at me as I was walked past like they knew exactly who I was.

The whole place was buzzing with military police, wounded, soldiers running everywhere, officers shouting commands, but there was no sense of panic. They knew the garrison would hold. Battered though it was, it was built to withstand anything the resistance could throw at it. Except they didn't know the KRM had a great huge siege engine of a mining robot.

I kept my head down. One of the MPs stopped us, protesting, trying to take hold of my shoulder. The sergeant stepped between us and squared up to the guy. I didn't catch everything he said, but he finished up clear enough with, "He's just a kid, and he's one of us." The MP muttered something, backed down and waved us through.

The sergeant was swearing to himself as he took me through to the medical centre and sat me in a seat in the corridor, staff hurrying past and no one taking any notice of us. He unfastened the cuffs, still looking like he didn't know how to speak to me.

I mumbled a thank you.

He stood and looked down at me. "Stay put, you understand?" he said and he left.

A medic came by after a while. I recognised her voice from when I was there before. She was the one that had argued with Charlie that they had to let me go.

She looked at me with dismay as she recognised me and was fraught as she checked me over, gentle as if she felt guilty about the state I was in, as if she wanted to say something about Charlie but didn't know how. I didn't know what to say either.

I looked up at her and said quietly, "There's a girl called Maisie…"

She shook her head without a word, checking my stats, not looking happy with whatever she was measuring, and giving me shots. I palmed an extra injector of painkillers from her tray while she was looking away and stashed it for later. I took the pass out of her pocket too. She told me they had shuttles in the courtyard, evacuating civilian staff and the worst of the wounded, and she told me to wait until she could get me a place on one. Then she left.

I had my way out but I wasn't going to take it alone.

It was way too busy for me to leave so I sat there, feeling the drugs kick in. I wanted to go find Maisie but every time I thought there might be a chance, more people would rush by. All the bays were full so they started to leave wounded in the corridor. Not all of them were soldiers. I stared, not wanting to look but wanting to know that none of them were people I knew.

The bombardment was so heavy now, some of the rockets were getting through the defence grid, the building shaking with each blast. The lights flickered. I hunkered there, on the verge of running out, when there was a direct hit overhead.

The corridor plunged into darkness. Debris rained down. I covered my head and ran.

24

There was another hit. The floor trembled. I ran, limping, holding onto anything that steadied my balance, through dark corridors, heading towards the lockup. Half the corridors were blocked by rubble.

I found a way through, ducked into a mostly intact office and used the medic's pass to access the base records through a terminal. The prisoner details were limited to stats, no names. It was going to take too long to scan through them and figure out which one was Maisie and which cell she was being held in so I opened all of them. I ditched the terminal and moved out, more cautiously as I approached the secure area, but there was another explosion, right on top of us.

I was thrown off my feet. I curled up and covered my head, coughing dust.

There was shouting, sounds of gunfire. The prisoners were running loose, fighting with the guards. I staggered to my feet and started to yell for Maisie, pushing past people who were running in the opposite direction. I heard her shout back, "Luka," then someone ran past me and shoved me aside. I fell.

There was a blast, a shockwave of pressure and darkness.

It was probably only for a second but I flashed right back to Rainfall. I was held there frozen in time, trapped, cold, and hurting so bad I couldn't even feel it any more. It was like I'd imagined the last eight years, dreamed up a life that hadn't happened, and I was still there, trapped under that building, and I couldn't breathe. But that time, the hand that reached for mine was warm and soft and it was Maisie who was calling my name. She brought me back. She pulled me clear and held onto me and I clung to her as she stroked the back of my neck.

"Are you hurt?"

I shook my head, coughed and gave her a grin. "I came to rescue you."

She laughed. "Nice rescue. How do we get away?"

Walking out of the front door wasn't an option.

"There are shuttles in the courtyard," I said. "They're evacuating the civilian staff. We just need to sneak on board."

We stood up. I wobbled, daggers stabbing into my knee. Maisie put her arm around my waist and I didn't complain. We just needed to avoid the fighting, hope another rocket didn't land on us and get the hell out.

We took a few steps towards what we thought was an empty corridor but there were shouts, beams of flashlights bouncing. We shrank back.

Maisie was clutching my hand, my arm draped around her neck. "You can hardly walk," she whispered. "Is there no other way?"

I shook my head. "We can't stay here. Come on, we just need to time it right."

We timed it really badly. We slipped out of a door and hugged the outside wall. The Imperial troops were regrouping. The courtyard was flooded with light from the towers, from hovering gunships, APCs moving into position with gun turrets and searchlights spinning. We could hear the hum of the powered armour of the heavy infantry as they set up portable auto sentries and mini-guns. They were getting ready to move out and push back against the onslaught.

We shrank into what shadow there was against the wall of the building. The air was heavy with dust and oil fumes. It was hard not to cough and I was starting to struggle just to stand. We could see the shuttles, one taking off as we watched, another with its ramp open and medics hustling. We just needed to get to it.

I squeezed Maisie's hand in readiness and opened my mouth to say, "Now," when there was a roar above. The defence grid was pounding at the incoming ordinance but the attack was relentless. A rocket made it through the grid and screamed in, exploding against an airborne gunship, chunks of burning metal flying out and cascading down in a billowing glow of orange. We flinched back from the heat, trying to shield each other, ears ringing.

There were shouts, screams.

It was our best chance.

I grabbed Maisie, whispered, "Go," and we stepped out, staying low.

I couldn't move fast enough. We took two steps and there was a yell.

Time froze.

I turned and looked right at the IDC guy. He was wearing full powered armour, standing there in the open, helmet in one hand, like he was invincible, a gun in his other hand. I had his access key in my pocket. We stared at each other for a heartbeat, rockets raining down on his base, the resistance forces pushing up in force, and the entire city rising against them. I could almost read his mind. I knew all his dirty little secrets and I would have bet my right arm that half the deals listed on that ledger were unsanctioned. If he wanted me dead, we were dead.

I grabbed Maisie's hand, ducked and ran.

We made it back inside, and round a corner, shots ricocheting off the walls next to us. We scrambled through another door. There was shouting behind us. I knew there was a maintenance access somewhere along that corridor but in the dark and with adrenaline pounding, I almost missed it. Maisie was all that was keeping me on my feet. I found the hatch, bust it open and pushed her in.

She wriggled through, twisting to look at me as I climbed in behind her, slamming the hatch shut and urging her forward. We made it up and into the twisted knotwork of cables before we heard the hatch open, cursing and shouting. He was screaming at us, yelling at his men to get us. There was no way they could follow us, not in powered armour, but they'd be able to track us.

I tugged on Maisie's ankle and crawled past her. We needed to move and we needed to move fast.

I led the way through the crawl spaces, feeling the walls tremble every time there was another hit. We could hear the distant echo of gunfire.

"How do we get out?" she whispered at me.

I turned back to her and shook my head. There was no way we'd be able to get out in one piece.

Not now.

"We don't," I said. "We go down."

I twisted and started to unstrap the brace from my knee. I could hardly move in there with it restricting the joint.

She didn't look impressed. "Down?"

"The tunnels go right under the base. There's one that goes to the space port from right under here."

You know I said she never questioned how I knew stuff. She did then. She blurted out, "How do you even know that?"

I screwed up my face. "You have to get under the AI core to get to it."

She pulled a face of her own. "What? You sure there's no other way?"

I couldn't think of one. We were cornered, the only way out was down.

Maisie struggled in a few places and I had to take it slower than I would usually but we made it round to the main manifold. Up was the comms centre, down was the command level and the AI core.

She leaned close as I wriggled into place and hacked into the garrison's control system.

"What are you doing?" she said as she watched.

I was scanning quickly through a sitrep. The AI was struggling. It was never expected to operate at the level it was currently being expected to. Kheris was a backwater, low threat rating. A full on assault on multiple targets was never considered in the possible scenarios it should have to deal with and for eight years it had never really been tested. Right then it was struggling and its learning algorithms were desperately trying to update and adapt to the worsening situation. But things were changing faster than it could keep up with. I felt torn. I wanted more than anything right then for the garrison to hold out and I didn't want to screw the AI up and risk tipping the balance but there was only one way out that I could think of.

"Finding us a way through," I muttered.

"What happened with Dayton's key?"

"Dayton's dead," I said as I worked. "He's been betraying us."

I felt her tremble.

"You killed him?"

"Calum killed him. Dayton's been working with the Empire this whole time. And at the end, he was even trying to sell them out to UM."

"Why?"

"Money." I didn't mention that I'd transferred it all to her. If we survived this, she'd find out.

I could almost feel the next question brewing before she asked it. "What about Benjie?"

"Same? I dunno." I was trying not to care. "You were right, he was just using me." I shifted my weight, pain flaring in my knee. "Listen, Spacey was evacuated. Peanut's waiting for us with a ship. I want you to come with us."

She was staring at me. She didn't say anything else but I could tell her mind was running at a million miles an hour. She went to speak a couple of times but stopped herself, finally just snapping Charlie's band off her wrist and back onto mine and keeping her hand there.

I gave the AI a few more problems to worry about, no need to screw with the power, half of it was out already. I did what I could, winging it to figure out a way down the levels, and wrapped up fast. My hands were shaking by the time I was done. We could hear the Imperial forces, distant sounds echoing as they tried to reach us, breaking in and shouting, hammering on the hatches and yelling warnings to stop or they'd open fire.

"Come on," I said, "we need to find the lift shaft."

I was reckoning that was our best bet to get down to the lower levels. I'd never tried it before.

I led the way, climbing through and squeezing past the thick knots of cable to get up into the comms centre where the lift shaft ended. That was the only way we could get in – get above it and drop down.

I found the access panel I was looking for and leaned in close to release the catch.

"Won't it know we're here?" Maisie whispered.

It. The AI.

"It's busy."

There was a chance it would but I'd sent enough conflicting reports and queries to it, in amongst all the damage reports and sitreps it was getting, that it wouldn't know what was what. It was trying to maintain the perimeter. It was holding. Just.

There was a clang and a hatch above us was ripped open.

I glanced up. A figure in powered armour burst in, flinging the hatch cover aside and roaring.

Maisie grabbed me and pulled me away as shots pinged off a pipe next to me. Steam hissed. I flinched back, shouldered the access panel open and pushed her through.

The air in the shaft was stale, cold. We clambered in, more shots hitting the walls around us. I risked reaching back, snatching the hatch shut behind us and flinching from shards of flying metal. It shut with a clang.

Maisie coughed, looking over my shoulder, hanging onto the ladder and leaning out, looking down. She swore. "Can you do this?" she breathed into my ear.

Dim lighting illuminated the shaft. The next access panel was half way down. I could just about see the top of the elevator at the bottom. My knee was throbbing again. I had no idea if I could make it but I nodded. "Race you to that panel."

She went and didn't look back. I ended up half falling down each rung of the ladder, balancing on my right leg and taking my weight on my arms. I had an increasing tickle at the back of my throat, a catch in my lungs that I knew was electrobes.

It was tough going. There was a sudden hum below me. I looked down. The lift was moving up, the noise from the mechanism getting louder. I wasn't going to make it. There was a clatter from above, pieces of panel went crashing past me and the entire lift shaft resounded with a deafening rattle of gunfire. Maisie started yelling. I dropped down a couple more rungs, trying to stay small and trying to move faster than my leg would let me. Something hot hit my hand with a burst of pain. I lost my grip and fell.

25

I tumbled, curled up and hit the top of the elevator as it rose to meet me. I hit it hard, breath driven from my lungs, shots punching down all around me. I scrambled to the side and crouched there, on the rising lift, flinching each time a shot came close, watching the access panel approach, feeling blood dripping off my hand, and clambered through as Maisie grabbed me, snatching my trailing foot out of the way as the lift continued on its way. She slammed the panel closed and held me, and we sat there clutching each other until I could breathe again.

"You're bleeding," she whispered.

I held out my hand, shaking. There was a ragged hole through it, oozing red. She pulled a cloth out of somewhere and bound it tight. I could hardly feel it. Charlie's band was tingling, numbers scrolling across its surface. I stifled a cough.

Maisie was struggling not to cough herself. "This is electrobes, isn't it?"

"Just ignore it," I whispered back. "If it gets that bad, we'll have to find some antidote somewhere."

She looked at me wide-eyed like I was mad.

"It never gets that bad," I lied. "Come on, we need to move. Stay close."

We climbed out and into the crawl space above the command level. There was a constant humming reverberation from the power plant and the AI core below us that was setting my nerves on edge.

I led her around to a vent and we slipped down, squeezing our way through, feeling the temperature go up and the noise increase. It seemed like madness to drop further down into the base but it was the only thing I could come up with. If we tried to run and make a break for the surface, they'd get us.

We squeezed through conduits from one crawl space to another until we were above the power plant, every inch tough going. I didn't care that I was leaving bloody handprints everywhere. The walls of the vent were vibrating, every noise banging through my head.

Maisie grabbed my arm. "You okay?"

I shook my head. My knee and my hand were hurting so bad the pain was making my stomach queasy. I fumbled in my pocket for the injector I'd lifted from the medic, almost dropping it, my hands were shaking that much. She took it from me and pressed it gently against my neck. It activated with a sting.

It was tempting to hold onto her and just sit there, rest my head against her shoulder and close my eyes.

She squeezed my left hand. "We need to go."

We dropped down into a dark corridor. Somewhere along the way, Maisie grabbed a length of bar and gave it to me to lean on. I shouldn't have taken the brace off my knee. She was holding me up and we half ran, half limped through the power plant, squeezing past cables and pipes, making our way through the open blast doors that separated each compartment, the noise so loud we didn't hear him come up behind us. A grenade clattered past, rolling, what light there was glinting off its surface. Maisie dropped me and ran right towards it, twisting and kicking it away. My leg gave way and I sprawled, seeing a looming figure in powered armour behind us as the grenade went spinning off, detonating with a flash. Stun grenades are nasty. Even catching the edge of it sent sparks flaring behind my eyes.

Maisie cursed and pulled me up and back into a stumbling run. I could hear him pounding up behind us.

We ran through the next blast door and I gasped, "Wait," pushing her to the side as I punched down on the door panel. He opened up on us, shots pinging past us down the corridor. I hunkered in close, shielding her and flinching as bullets ricocheted off the wall next to us. One of the thick overhead conduits above us exploded, a sickly green glow of steam and vapour showering down as the door slammed shut. It felt like I was inhaling lungfuls of tiny, razor sharp, superheated pins. The band on my wrist started vibrating like it was about to explode. Maisie was coughing. I pulled off the door panel and yanked out wires, shorting out the controls and glancing back through the sealed air-tight door as the massive figure thundered up and started to pound on it with his armoured fist.

There was a manual release. I saw him reaching for it,

grabbed the bar and stuck it through the handle on our side, jamming it tight. It would hold, but not for long.

I turned.

Maisie was doubled over.

"Luka, go," she gasped.

"I'm not leaving you," I muttered, grabbed her arm and pulled her up and forward. Another conduit overhead exploded in a shower of sparks and green vapour. We ran through it, stumbling towards the next blast door. A siren started screaming, emergency lights flashing red. I could see the warning lights, hear the mechanism whirr. Flares of light were flickering across my eyes. We couldn't move fast enough. My knee gave way. Maisie pushed me before I could stop her. I stumbled forward and fell.

The door slammed closed.

I got to my knees and turned, cold. She was on the other side. I could see her on the floor. The alarm was still shrieking. I shouted and screamed, pounding at the door and the release panel but it wouldn't open.

It felt like I'd been kicked in the chest. I couldn't let it happen again.

I turned and ran.

There was only one way I could get that door to open. I could hardly breathe and that was nothing to do with the electrobe poisoning. I found a maintenance hatch, bust it open with trembling fingers that were slick with blood and worked my way through and down, falling as much as climbing, an icy vein of panic clutching at my stomach.

The band around my forearm was still vibrating with what I guessed was a warning that the electrobe concentration was bad enough to be beyond shit.

The level housing the AI core was quieter, the droning hum of the power plant above just a distant reverberation. I made my way through it, running on pure adrenaline. They couldn't track me down there. There's so much interference around an AI, there was no way they could have tracked the lifesigns of a horde of invaders. I saw a bunch of technicians in environment suits but it wasn't hard to avoid them.

I didn't have much of a plan, and from the burning in my chest I didn't have much time, but it didn't need any finesse. All AI cores, even the old ones, are protected from meltdowns and outside attack. That's why they're usually buried so deep. No one ever anticipated someone being stupid enough to climb into one though.

I found the interface that led to the main manifold for the cooler system surrounding the core, hacked open the control panel and slipped inside.

The sound was deafening. My heart was beating in time with the thrumming din. The cables were pulsing. Tiny remote maintenance drones were buzzing around in all directions. I could feel the electrobes in every breath, every blink. My skin was crawling.

I reached out my left hand, fingers spread wide, and touched a conduit that was warm and soft.

This was a main artery that fed the thing that had killed Charlie. And now it was killing Maisie. I know there are places that recognise AIs as sentient. To me, it was a machine and it was programmed to be vicious and ruthless and murdering. I didn't care whose side it was on. I knew what the consequences of what I was planning would be. With the AI gone, the whole base would be in chaos, the defence grid would be down and without the automated defences, the garrison would fall. You ever heard of the Kheris massacre? Well, that was all down to me. But right then I didn't care. I've done a lot of stuff in my time with the guild, but that night…? It was either my best or my worst. All I wanted to do was get Maisie to safety.

I pulled out Charlie's knife and gnawed away at the cables with the blade until I had enough bare wires exposed that they started to spark. The air around me erupted. I was knocked back and sent sprawling as the cables caught fire, the electrobes in the air flaring and dying with a flurry of brilliant light as it set off a chain reaction.

I can remember thinking that was probably enough.

Then the whole compartment blew.

I was thrown backwards. I curled up and shielded my head, fingers burned and nerve endings raw. Alarms were screaming, the sound distorted and far off. I crawled back to the interface, scrambled through and pushed myself to my feet.

And looked up into the sights of a hunter killer drone, right there, hovering at head height.

It was spinning, scanning round. It stopped, homed in on me, weapons bearing round, and shifted so fast, it was inches from my face before I could move.

There was nowhere to go, nowhere to hide. This was it. Its actuators were humming as it adjusted its aim, its laser targeting system shining red between my eyes. In all the times I'd raided the garrison, I'd never seen one active in there. They'd sent it after me.

I froze, waiting for the shot.

It backed up and dropped to chest height. I tensed, staring at it, chin up, defying it to kill me. An arc of fine blue beams speared out of it and danced over me, scanning. They focused in on the tags around my neck and shut off abruptly. The drone spun and shot off, hunting down the next life signs it could detect.

I reached for the chain, Charlie's tags, and stood there like an idiot, staring after it, still not breathing and starting to tremble.

Another compartment inside the core blew. I was on my knees before I knew what was happening. The heat was immense. I covered my head and crawled through broken glass and shards of plastic that burned into my skin.

I made it to the hatch and climbed back up to the power plant.

The blast doors were closed, the conduits still spewing out green vapour. The alarm had changed to a wailing siren and an automated message calling for immediate evacuation. I hit the release button and that time there was no AI to countermand the instruction. The door opened.

Maisie was sitting with her eyes closed, head leaned forward against the wall. She wasn't moving. I scrambled down next to her, a cold knot twisting in my stomach, but she twitched as I reached for her, swore and jerked upright, grabbing my arm.

She coughed.

The level was filling with smoke fast. There was a crash and a bang at the other door, yells. They were still trying to get through.

I pulled her up and we moved, both of us doubled over coughing, me limping and half blind with the pain. There was no way we had time to make it to the tunnel entrance. But there was another route. We were screwed anyway. I took her straight down through the burning AI core and into the substructure beneath the whole garrison. I couldn't tell what was worse after a while, the heat, the pain in my knee and hand, the electrobes in my chest or that dull droning vibration that was almost subliminal in its intensity.

Whole compartments were collapsing around us. Sections blowing out. Pipes and conduits buckling. I don't even know how we found the tunnel access but we dropped down into a chill, damp space and let the hatch slam shut above us, shutting out the heat and noise with a bang.

It opened out into a tunnel. The air was stale but breathable so there must have been some kind of ventilation.

Maisie was struggling to keep herself upright but she grabbed my arm and hoisted it over her shoulder, slipping the other around my waist again.

She made a choking gesture around her throat as we moved as fast as we could manage, and whispered, "I take it this is bad?"

I nodded. I coughed, chest hurting. If you've ever had electrobe poisoning beyond critical, you'll understand how much it hurt. I didn't know if my eyes were watering from the pain or the electrobes. The band on my forearm had stopped vibrating. It was just humming, constricted tight. I had a feeling that was a bad sign.

We could hear the explosions above us. Part of the tunnel ceiling up ahead started to rain dust and debris, the steel wall supports groaning, starting to bend.

We couldn't move any faster. Maisie lost her balance and we stumbled, staggering, almost going down, desperately trying to hold each other up.

There was a noise way back in the tunnel. Distant voices echoed, a faint clatter of armour and weapons.

We turned, staring.

They were trying every possible way to get in, to get to us.

Another reverberating shockwave behind us sent dust flying past. I flinched and glanced back. The tunnel was going to collapse. We were going to be trapped and caught or buried alive. I didn't know which would be worse.

26

We didn't stand there to wait and see. We turned and staggered back into a run, stumbling towards the collapsing section of tunnel.

The pressure against my chest was getting worse. I could feel Maisie getting heavier and heavier against my arm. Chunks of the tunnel lining were crashing down. We ducked falling concrete, clambered over rubble and dragged each other through the narrowing gap, tumbling and sprawling clear as the roof came down behind us in a billowing cloud of dust.

I pushed to my elbows and looked back. It was only partially blocked but there was no way they'd get through that easily in powered armour. And from what I knew of the plans, there was no other way in to this tunnel. They'd have to clear a way through to get to us.

Maisie coughed. She looked up at me, tears welling. She was shaking.

I crawled to her and hugged her tight.

I pulled back and looked at her, so close our noses were almost touching. She moved towards me and I thought she was going to kiss me, but she put her finger against my lips and just breathed, "Kiss me when we're out of here."

I could hardly speak, throat beyond dry, but I nodded and croaked, "Race you to the end?"

She managed a smile and we staggered up and on.

We were almost on our knees when we hit the end of the tunnel. I pushed her up the ladder ahead of me and we emerged into warm, clean air, and chaos. I squinted, shielding my eyes. It was bright outside, the rising sun already high. The sky was full, ships taking off, gunships and drop ships buzzing over the space port. The noise of vehicles and voices from the gate was at fever pitch. Deep rumblings and the sound of explosions were carrying from the direction of the garrison.

I twisted around to look. Smoke was billowing out across the entire skyline as the KRM bombed the Imperial stronghold and took out every outpost. I didn't find out until later how bad it was. It wouldn't be long before the onslaught reached the space port. And this base hardly had any defences. The panic to get out was overwhelming.

Maisie sank down to the ground. We weren't far from the medical centre. I couldn't get her to her feet, couldn't gather the strength to lift her, every muscle screaming, too close to dropping myself.

I squeezed her hand and gasped, "Wait here."

I didn't even know if she heard me. She didn't respond. I dragged myself away from her, limping, stumbling, towards the emergency room.

There was no one there. They'd abandoned the place already. I pushed my way through and slipped into a side room, rifled through drawers and threw dressings and jars aside, no idea where they'd keep any antidote. I leaned on the counter, vision narrowed to a dark tunnel, looked up and saw that sweet little label on a box in a glass cabinet. It was locked. I smashed my elbow through it, grabbed the box and tumbled out the single injector left in it.

There was only one dose.

My hands were shaking.

I turned and ran, staggering back out into the open.

It felt like time slowed.

I could see Peanut waving at me from across the compound, there was shouting from the other side, powered armour-clad soldiers emerging from the tunnel. And Maisie was lying out there on the tarmac.

I had one dose of antidote clutched in numb fingers.

I looked at Peanut. He had the courier ship out from its maintenance bay, engines fired up, and he was standing on the ramp, gesturing at me like mad to get over there. I didn't know if he could even see Maisie. He shouted again, yelling to me to get to him. That was my chance to get away.

I looked across to the other side. The guy in black was striding across the tarmac. He had his helmet in his hand, face like thunder.

There was no way I could leave Maisie.

I looked from Peanut to the IDC guy again and back to Maisie. She wasn't moving.

I staggered out to her and sank down beside her, heart pounding, trying to feel for a pulse, and fumbling the vial of antidote in fingers that felt like lead. She wasn't breathing. I injected it into her neck and held her tight. I couldn't even feel if her heart was beating, mine was pounding so hard. I cradled her there, my head against hers, tears streaming down my face, hearing the shouts getting closer.

I couldn't lose her. After everything we'd been through, I couldn't bear to lose Maisie as well. I stroked the hair back from her face, not caring that I was dying there with her.

Footsteps thundered up, weapons clattering. They were on me in seconds, dragged me away from her and threw me forward.

My knees hit the dust and I almost sprawled except someone grabbed the back of my shirt and hauled me upright. They grabbed my arms and pulled my hands behind my back, restraints clamping my wrists tight.

I squinted, head pounding, stumbling as they pushed me forward. The bindings were cutting into my skin. My knee had gone. I couldn't put any weight on it at all. And the pressure in my chest was almost unbearable.

I tried to twist round to see Maisie but they wouldn't let me.

It was quiet.

For a second.

Then they started shouting, searching me roughly, hitting me about the head and emptying my pockets, throwing all my stuff onto the ground in front of me, kicking it around to see what it was as if they didn't want to touch any of it, screaming at me the whole time, yelling right in my ear.

I didn't listen to what they were saying. They shouted louder but I zoned it all out and didn't fight them. I'd trashed their AI and left them wide open to attack from an enemy that was in frenzy, the entire colony rising against them. To say they were pissed and to say I was screwed was the understatement of the century.

I knelt there in the dust, agonising waves pulsing up and down my leg, hands tied behind my back, head down and a gun barrel pressed against the back of my head.

End of the line.

Not exactly Latia's firing squad against the wall but not far from it.

I could almost feel the finger trembling on its trigger, almost see the look of disappointment in Latia's eyes. I was glad Charlie wasn't there to see me like that.

The IDC guy leaned down in front of me and picked the key out of the dust. "Bad mistake, kid," he said. "Kill him." And he walked away towards his ship.

The soldiers tensed. Someone grabbed my shoulder, hard, and the gun pushed, forcing my head down.

I closed my eyes.

Then someone shouted.

I was vaguely aware of vehicles pulling up and skidding to a halt all around us, wheels kicking out dust, and doors slamming. There were more shouts, someone ordering them to stand down, barking at them, and I felt them back off, even the pressure of the gun against my head easing back slightly.

Footsteps crunched up ahead of us. I squinted, blinking dust out of my eyes, to see boots, uniforms.

They stopped.

The same someone gave a command to get me up, a quiet voice but loaded with so much authority that they hustled, helping me up and even dusting me off. I had to balance on my right leg and they had to keep hold of me to stop me sinking back to the ground. I kept my head down but I looked up, eyes hooded, not sure if this was a reprieve or something worse.

Whoever it was stepped forward. He wasn't a big man, not like most of the soldiers, but he had a presence about him, dark eyes that were piercing with a glint in them that made me dare think this might be okay.

He looked at me for a long time, what felt like forever.

"You get to choose," he said.

And it felt like everyone else disappeared, faded out into the background, and it was only me and this man standing there in the heat of the sun. I still had my arms restrained behind my back, chest wheezing with every breath.

"You come with me, right now," he said, "or you get a bullet in the back of the head, right now."

I stared at him.

He had the sleeves of his fatigues rolled up, Earth Marine Corps uniform, colonel's tags on his arm and a black band like Charlie's around his wrist. He lowered his voice even though it felt like there was only me that could hear. "Understand this," he said. "You choose to come with me? We go now. You do not get to say goodbye to anyone, you do not get to take anything with you. You cease to exist. You will never return to Kheris. Do you understand?"

I couldn't move.

"Or I give them the go ahead to shoot you."

My head was pounding with every heartbeat.

"What is it to be?"

It was an impossible choice. It was everything I wanted. But not just for me, never just for me.

He made it easy.

He leaned close. "You make the right choice, I can make sure that girl over there gets out of this alive. She'll be fine. Your great-grandmother will be fine. That kid over there who was about to steal a ship for you… will be fine. Be smart, Luka, now of all times. Think about it."

He stepped back.

I nodded, heart in my stomach, but I nodded.

And that's how I met Mendhel Halligan.

He said something I didn't catch and the soldiers around me hustled again, freeing my hands.

I doubled over, coughing, dry retching, and he caught hold of my arm and turned it, looking at the numbers scrolling on the band there.

He cursed, dropped my arm and caught up the dog tags around my neck, holding them in his palm and looking at them for a second before swearing again. He turned to walk away, beckoning me to follow as he went back to the vehicle. I could hardly walk but someone ran up and helped me get there, sitting me down and popping injector after injector into my neck.

The pressure in my chest started to ease straight away. Antidote. "Maisie," I said without thinking, panicking, "She…"

He interrupted with a curt, "She'll be fine." He turned to the woman who was checking me over. "Is he good to go?"

I was trying not to react as she pulled the rag off my right hand even though it took a chunk of flesh with it. She sprayed it with something and tied a clean bandage around it, then wrapped some kind of field dressing around my leg, pulling it tight, a warm pressure easing the pain.

It felt too good to be true. And the whole time, Maisie was lying out there and I had no idea if she was even still alive.

"He's as good as he's going to get," the woman said. "This knee needs surgery. And the hand is a mess. We'll need to quarantine. Same as the other kid."

The colonel didn't look impressed and muttered under his breath.

"Are we going in now?" she said to him, peering into my eyes with some kind of bright light that stung like a bitch.

I flinched away.

She checked my pulse again, speaking to the guy as if I wasn't there. "He needs a medevac. You want me to let Control know?"

I suddenly, more than anything, needed to go back to Maisie, even if just for a second. I blurted out, "Wait," before I realised what I was doing.

They both looked at me like I was some stray dog that had just spoken.

I was close to tears. "There's something I need to do."

"I said no goodbyes," the man said, moving to close the door.

"It's not a goodbye, I swear. It's something I need to do." I've never needed anything so much in my entire life. My heart was thumping.

I thought he was going to pull me out of the vehicle and throw me to the ground, fire that bullet into my head himself.

He didn't.

He closed the door and climbed into the front. The woman got into the driver's seat.

"No goodbyes," he said again. "You are going to have to learn to listen to me, Mr Anderton."

I couldn't help reaching for the dog tags.

He looked back at me. "We need to call you something. LC Anderton will do just fine. Charlie was one of our best. I expect you to live up to his name."

I looked back out of the window as we drove off. Maisie was still lying on the ground, medics buzzing around her. The soldiers were backing off, guns held down, boots kicking up dust, as the medics worked on her. Her face was pale, one hand outstretched.

I could see her hair, soft curls black against the red dirt.
We drove away.
And that was the last time I saw her.
I never did get to give her that kiss.

There was another kid on the ship they took me to. They helped me on board and steered me to a seat. They hadn't given me any more drugs.

I didn't recognise the type of ship. It wasn't any kind of Imperial military spec I was familiar with, there were no insignia, no badges, nothing to identify it at all. It was clean, spotlessly clean, and just the right level of warm. The seat was comfortable, the lighting soft, the gravity light enough to make me feel like I was floating. It didn't feel real.

The woman squeezed my shoulder and, finally, popped a couple more shots into my neck. She leaned in close and whispered into my ear, "Welcome home," before she walked forward to take a seat.

I stared at the kid opposite. He looked a bit older than me, dark hair shaved close to his head, black bruising under one eye and a set to his jaw like he was expecting a fight and wasn't sure which direction it was going to come from.

He looked up at me, wary.

I had a feeling I was looking at him the same way.

Mendhel was stripping off his uniform. He threw the

jacket into a waste disposal unit and walked between us. "LC, this is Hilyer. Hil, LC. Welcome to the Thieves' Guild."

"And that's how I ended up in the most secretive guild in the galaxy."

The candle has burned down to a nub. I watch Luka take a swig of liquor from his flask and give it a shake. I can tell there's not much left. He drinks too much. But who can blame him for that?

It's been over ten years since that night on Kheris. I know he's never talked about it before. To anyone. I don't know why he's telling us now. Maybe to say there's always a way out. However bad it seems to be.

These kids, huddled with us in this dark basement, are staring at him with their cold little faces, and I know exactly what they're thinking… he wasn't much older than most of them when he did it, even younger than some. Even now, he's not that different, at least not in some ways.

I don't know how much longer he can keep them quiet. I can hear sporadic gunfire in the distance, that guttural roar of troop carriers overhead that makes him shiver when he thinks no one is watching.

"What happened then?" one of the little ones says.

Luka shrugs. "Mendhel took us to the Alsatia and we ran riot. The guild was never set up to take kids. I didn't know it at the time but Mendhel put himself on the line doing what he did that day. There was no way back for any of us."

I look up. I can hear drop ships descending right above us.

Luka catches my eye and nods.

A cold knot twists in my stomach. I hope they're ours. I know he doesn't have much ammunition left.

He makes a move to stand, but one of the kids touches his arm and whispers, "Tell us about the time you broke into Yarrimer."

Another one pipes up, "And Polaris."

He grins. That's one thing that hasn't changed.

"That was all back when we were invincible," he says, "when we were chasing for the top and the standings were all that mattered. But those stories'll have to wait for another day."

"What do we do now?" one of them asks.

I watch as he checks the mechanism on his rifle. That's what is different. Luka was never a soldier. Now he carries a gun and he carries scars that none of us will ever understand.

"Now?" he says. "Now we survive." He stands and starts to move them out, herding them ahead of him, this rag-tag bunch of kids in misfitting thrown-together body armour that he managed to get here to safety. We lost a couple when it got really bad. They might be out there somewhere, safe in some other place with someone, but I doubt it.

I stop him on the stairs and hand him his helmet.

He gives me a smile. "Cheers, Spacey."

He promised me that night on Kheris that he'd come find me. It took over ten years but he did. He always keeps his promises. And he saved us out there tonight.

I can't help asking, "Will we?"

He looks puzzled. "Will we what?"

"Survive," I say simply.

He shrugs again. "We have so far…"

We can hear shouts echo down from above us, familiar voices, guild voices.

I smile back. "Do you promise?"

———————

Also by C.G. Hatton
available from Sixth Element Publishing
in paperback and eBook

BEYOND REDEMPTION
LC BOOK TWO

The infamous Thieves' Guild, the most secretive organisation in the galaxy, doesn't recruit kids... and with good reason. But now circumstances force their hand.

When an undercover operation goes wrong, they have no choice but to bring in two potential recruits they've been watching. Pulled from the chaos of the rebellion on Kheris, Luka finds himself thrown into the intense arena of field-op training alongside Zach Hilyer, another kid with a troubled past.

Still struggling with injuries, and sent into a place far more dangerous than even the guild realises, Luka doesn't know who he can trust and has no way out. The stakes rise fast, and he is faced with a decision that could prove fatal for them both.

"Excellent sequel to Kheris Burning,
I couldn't put this book down til the end."

"Written with the joy of a storyteller's soul,
fast-paced, surprising and full of the unexpected..."

Also by C.G. Hatton
available from Sixth Element Publishing
in paperback and eBook

DEFYING WINTER
LC BOOK THREE

LC Anderton, raw recruit and thief-in-training, is struggling at the Thieves' Guild.

Screwing up is second nature for LC and when he gets into trouble yet again, he's sent off on a minor assignment to get him out of the way. Only this time he's got his eye on a different mission, a mission no other field-op in the guild will touch. Because it's impossible. And to LC, that's a challenge he can't resist. But it's impossible for a reason, and LC isn't the only one after it. As the odds stack up against him, he can walk away or go all in... but even he can't imagine what will be asked of him and the price he'll have to pay.

"A story that defines LC as a field op, a story that at times had me on the edge of my seat and other times in tears as he beats the odds stacked against him."

"Fast-paced sci fi at its best. Written with passion and flair, this is a book that's hard to put down once you start reading because every chapter hangs you over a cliff."

*Also by C.G. Hatton
available from Sixth Element Publishing
in paperback and eBook*

RESIDUAL BELLIGERENCE
THIEVES' GUILD BOOK ONE

Zach Hilyer is in trouble. Taking a package from A to B always gets more complicated when A doesn't want to lose it and C will pay and do anything to get their hands on it. Hil is good, one of the best field operatives in the guild.

Problem is, he can't remember when it all went wrong. After crash landing on a planet with no memory of his last assignment, Hil discovers that his handler is dead and someone's put a price on his head. Injured and alone, he has no choice but to go rogue from the guild, fight to clear his name and wreak revenge on the people who set him up.

"I could not put this book down...
Quick descriptions, great dialogue as well
as wonderful story lines."

"This book rocks! I loved the way the story's
universe starts out lived in and established.
Fantastic sci-fi with tons of action. I can't wait
to continue the series."

Also by C.G. Hatton
available from Sixth Element Publishing
in paperback and eBook

BLATANT DISREGARD
THIEVES' GUILD BOOK TWO

LC Anderton is running out of places to hide. He's the best operative the Thieves' Guild has ever had... or at least he was until he screwed up his last job, the one he was blackmailed into taking. And that's just the start of his problems.

The entire galaxy wants the package he stole and will pay any price to get it. As bounty hunters close in, LC doesn't know who he can trust. In desperation, he throws in his lot with the chaotic crew of a rundown freighter on the edge of colonised space. And from there, it can only get worse.

Amidst the growing threat of war between Earth and Winter, the Thieves' Guild is desperate to find LC before anyone else can get their hands on him. The trouble is, he doesn't trust them either.

"Another fast-paced and exciting installment of the Thieves' Guild... I can't wait for the next one!"

"Fast moving, action-filled sci-fi from CG Hatton, with great, intriguing characters..."

Also by C.G. Hatton
available from Sixth Element Publishing
in paperback and eBook

HARSH REALITIES
THIEVES' GUILD BOOK THREE

Someone is out to destroy the Thieves' Guild. NG is good. Very good. But now someone wants him dead. With the guild in chaos, his best handler murdered and his top field-ops on the run, he has to up his game to find out who. Because that's only half the trouble he's in. As the cracks grow ever wider, the Thieves' Guild finds itself caught between the warring factions of Earth and Winter, with no idea who is pulling the strings. And on the darkest of days, NG finds himself in a fight even he couldn't have anticipated.

"I finished book three yesterday and loved it and I'm even more eager for the next in the series. Thanks for the great characters and stories, it's been a long time since I read any books as original and gripping as these."

"Awesome. I love the way it's tying all the convergent lines together…"

Also by C.G. Hatton
available from Sixth Element Publishing
in paperback and eBook

WILFUL DEFIANCE
THIEVES' GUILD BOOK FOUR

For someone who's supposed to be dead, NG is causing a lot of trouble. Haunted by nightmares of the alien invaders, he cares about only one thing – isolating a strain of the elusive virus that could give humans their only chance to fight back. But he's not the only one after it.

In a race against time and in a battle with his inner demons, he makes a grave mistake. And it is one that could cost the human race everything. The entire galaxy is in turmoil, the guild is in pieces and NG is the only one who can save them. But who will save him?

"Book four of the Thieves' Guild was amazing. Fast paced and full of twists and turns. I couldn't put it down and often read late into the night. Where to from this desperate position? Can't wait for book 5!"

"Great series... Fantastic set of books, I was hooked at the first book and look forward to seeing what happens to the characters in the next installment."

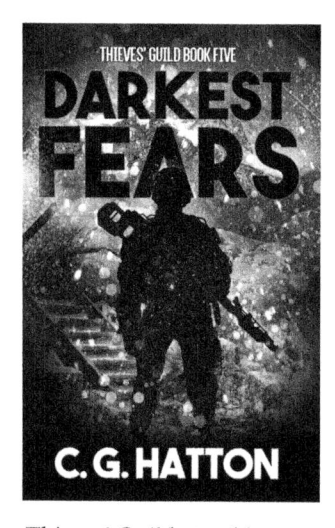

Also by C.G. Hatton
available from Sixth Element Publishing
in paperback and eBook

DARKEST FEARS
THIEVES' GUILD BOOK FIVE

The galaxy is at war... it's just not the war anyone expected.

Faced with an onslaught the like of which has never been seen before, only the remnants of the mythical Thieves' Guild stand between survival and extinction at the hands of an alien horde.

Taken captive by the ruthless invaders, thief turned reluctant soldier LC Anderton has only one priority – survive long enough to rescue NG, head of the Thieves' Guild who is missing in action and their only chance to turn the tide. But LC is fighting his own war, and it's one he's not sure he can win.

"WOW! Just WOW! The writing is fast-paced, which is characteristic of this universe of books (yes this is now a universe, not a trilogy - yay!)"

"Awesome twists, non-stop action, really cool characters and the world completely absorbs you! Great addition to the series!"

Also by C.G. Hatton
available from Sixth Element Publishing
in paperback and eBook

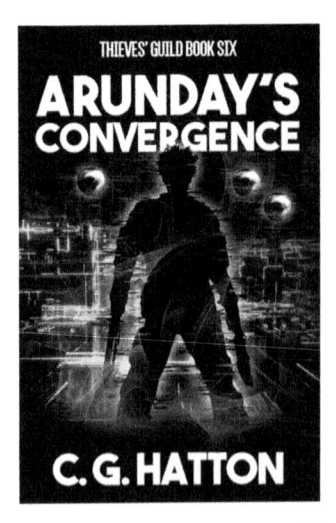

ARUNDAY'S CONVERGENCE
THIEVES' GUILD BOOK SIX

The war against the alien horde is all but lost... human-occupied space is overrun while the Thieves' Guild tries desperately to hold together a fragile alliance of Earth and Wintran resistance.

As the freak mutation of the alien virus continues to ravage his body, Zach Hilyer can't be detected by the telepathic invaders. And with NG and LC out of the picture, he's the most powerful remaining weapon the guild has against the Bhenykhn. Their only weapon.

Sent ever deeper into enemy territory on mission after mission, the demands of the Thieves' Guild, the resistance and the Seven super AIs are pushing him to breaking point. But Hil isn't just hiding from the aliens. His greatest fear isn't losing the war, it's losing himself.

"CG Hatton is as ever on top form, raising the high bar ever higher."

"All the fast paced action, hanging by your fingernails peril you would expect from CG Hatton."

Also available from Sixth Element Publishing and including Thieves' Guild short stories:

HARVEY DUCKMAN PRESENTS...

Harvey Duckman presents the first in a series of collected works of suspense and mystery in the genres of science fiction, fantasy, horror and steampunkery, called, oddly enough Harvey Duckman Presents…

This anthology features work by exciting new voices in speculative fiction, including both established authors and previously unpublished writers. These short stories give a glimpse into some fantastic worlds that are already out there for you to enjoy, as well as a taste of more to come.

Volume 1 includes stories by: Kate Baucherel, D.W. Blair, A.L. Buxton, Joseph Carrabis, R. Bruce Connelly, Nate Connor, Marios Eracleous, Craig Hallam, C.G. Hatton, Mark Hayes, Peter James Martin, Reino Tarihmen, J.L. Walton, Graeme Wilkinson and Amy Wilson.
Edited by C.G. Hatton.

"A great collection for anyone who likes science fiction, steampunk or just plain weird stories…"

FIND OUT MORE AT
WWW.CGHATTON.COM

Printed in Great Britain
by Amazon